FIGHTING
for RAIN

Jill -
Just keep fighting!

BB Easton

ISBN: 978-1-7327007-4-1
e-book ISBN: 978-1-7327007-5-8

Cover Design by BB Easton
Cover Photographs licensed by Adobe Stock
Content Editing by Traci Finlay and Karla Nellenbach
Copyediting by Jovana Shirley of Unforeseen Editing
and Ellie McLove of My Brother's Editor
Formatting by Jovana Shirley of Unforeseen Editing

*This book is dedicated to anyone who was ever afraid
but did the damn thing anyway.
Especially you, Staci.*

Fighting for Rain
Synopsis

THE WORLD WAS SUPPOSED to end on April 23, but Rainbow Williams's world ended days before that. The mass hysteria caused by the impending apocalypse claimed everything she'd ever loved. Her family. Her city. Her will to live.

Until she met *him*.

Wes Parker didn't have anything left for the apocalypse to take … he'd already lost it all by the time he was nine years old. His family. His home. His hope of ever being loved.

Until he met *her*.

Brought together by fate and bound by a love that would last lifetimes, Rain and Wes were prepared to die together on April 23.

They were not prepared for what would happen on *April 24.*

April 24, 1:35 a.m.
Rain

WITH MY ARMS AROUND Wes's waist and the roar of a motorcycle engine drowning out my thoughts, I turn and watch my house disappear behind us. My home. The only one I've ever known. The trees and darkness swallow it whole as we speed away, but they don't take my memories of what happened there. I wish they would. I wish I could pull this ache out of my chest and throw it into that house like a hand grenade.

I also wish I weren't wearing this damn motorcycle helmet. Wes should be wearing it. He's the survivalist. I don't really care if my head gets cracked open. All I want to do is lay my cheek on his back and let the wind dry my tears. Besides, the inside of it smells like hazelnut coffee and cold-cream moisturizer. Just like my mama.

Who's now buried in a shallow grave behind that house.

Right beside the man who killed her.

I might have survived April 23, but not all of me made it out alive. Rainbow Williams—the perfectly preppy, straight A–earning, churchgoing, trophy girlfriend of Franklin Springs High School basketball star Carter Renshaw—is buried back there too, right next to the parents she was trying so hard to please.

All that's left of me now is Rain.

Whoever the hell that is.

I curl my fingers into Wes's blue Hawaiian shirt and look over his shoulder at the black highway laid out before us. My friends, Quint and Lamar, are up ahead in their daddy's bulldozer, clearing a path through all the wrecked and abandoned vehicles that piled up during the chaos before April 23, but it's so dark that I can barely see them. All I can see is the road directly in front of our headlight and a few sparks in the distance where the bulldozer's blade is grinding against the asphalt. All I can smell are my memories. All I can feel is Wes's warm body in my arms and a sense of freedom in my soul, growing with every mile we put between us and Franklin Springs.

And, right now, that's all I need.

The rumble of the road and the emotional exhaustion of the past few days have me fighting to keep my eyes open. I nod off, I don't even know how many times, as we crawl along behind the bulldozer, jerking awake the moment I feel that first twitch of sleep.

Wes slows to a stop so that he can turn to face me. A lock of hair falls over one cheek, but the rest is pushed straight back and tangled from the wind. His pale green eyes are almost the only feature I can make out in the dark. And they don't look too happy.

"You're scaring the shit out of me. You've got to try to stay awake, okay?" Wes shouts over the sound of metal scraping asphalt up ahead.

I glance past him and see the headlights of the bulldozer shining on the roof of an overturned eighteen-wheeler. It's blocking the entire highway, but Quint and Lamar are hard at work, trying to push it out of our path.

I pull Mama's helmet off my head and feel her disappear along with her scent. It's replaced with the smell of spring pollen, pine trees, and gasoline.

"I know," I shout back with a guilty nod. "I'm trying."

A burst of sparks flies behind Wes as the bulldozer gives the tractor-trailer another good shove.

Wes puts the kickstand down and gets off the bike. "This is gonna take them a while. Maybe you should stand up and walk around a little. Might help you wake up."

He's just a silhouette, backlit by the haze from the headlight, but he's still the most beautiful thing I've ever seen—tall and strong and smart and *here*, even after everything he just witnessed. As I place my palm in his, the tiny orange sparkles of light glittering in the background match the ones dancing across my skin, giving me goose bumps, even under my hoodie.

I can't see his expression, but I feel Wes smiling down at me. Then, suddenly, his energy shifts. As I slide off the bike, he grips my hand tighter, lifting his head and inhaling so deeply that I can hear it, even over the grinding, crunching sounds coming from the bulldozer.

"Shit." The profile of his perfect face comes into view as he turns his head to look over his shoulder. "I think I smell—"

Before the word can even leave Wes's lips, the eighteen-wheeler explodes in a ball of fire. White-hot light fills my eyes and scorches my face as Wes tackles me to the ground.

I don't feel the impact. I don't hear the debris landing all around us. I don't even hear my own voice as I shout my friends' names. All I can hear are the thoughts in my head, telling me to get up. To run. To help.

Wes is looking down at me now. His lips are moving, but I can't tell what he's saying. Another explosion goes off, and I cover my face. When I lower my hands, he's gone.

I sit up and see Wes's silhouette running toward the bulldozer.

Which is now engulfed in flames.

"Quint!" I scream, taking off in a sprint toward the passenger side as Wes heads toward the driver's side. "Lamar!"

I climb up onto the track, thanking God that the fire hasn't made it through the blown-out windshield yet, and pull the door open. Inside, Quint and Lamar are slumped over in their seats, covered in broken glass. Wes is unbuckling Quint's seat belt. His head snaps up when I open the door, and his dark eyebrows pull together.

"I told you to stay the fuck there!"

"I couldn't hear you!" I lean into the cab, struggling to move Lamar's body so that I can unbuckle his seat belt.

"Rain, stop!" Wes snaps at me as he lifts Quint's lifeless body into his arms.

"I can help!" I get the belt off and give Lamar's shoulder a hard shake. His eyes flutter open as something begins to hiss and pop under the flaming hood. "Come on, buddy. We gotta go."

Lamar twists in his seat to try to climb out, but he winces and pulls his eyes shut again.

"Lamar," I shout, tugging on his shoulders. "I need you to walk. Right now."

His head rolls toward me, and the light from the flames illuminates a deep gash across his forehead. The dark red blood glistens against his dark brown skin. I pull on his arms harder, but he's so heavy.

"Lamar! Wake up! Please!"

Two hands clamp around my waist and pull me out of the cab just before a blur of Hawaiian print swoops in to take my place.

"Go!" Wes shouts as he pulls Lamar from the bulldozer. "Now!"

I jump off the track to get out of his way and run toward the motorcycle. As I get closer, I notice Quint's body lying on the ground next to it.

It isn't moving.

As I rush to him, my mind goes back to the day we met. We were in the same preschool class, and I found Quint off by himself on the first day of school, quietly eating Play-Doh behind Ms. Gibson's desk. He begged me not to tell on him. I didn't, of course. Instead, I sat and ate some with him just to see what all the fuss was about.

I found out years later that his daddy used to beat him whenever he got in trouble, so he got real good at not getting caught. His little brother, Lamar, didn't seem to learn the same lesson. He got caught all the time, but Quint always took the blame.

I kneel next to my very first friend and reach for his throat, hoping to find a pulse, but I don't get that far. I find a shard of glass sticking out of his neck instead.

"Oh my God." The words fall from my mouth as I grab his wrist, pushing and prodding and praying for a heartbeat.

Wes sets Lamar down next to me as another explosion rattles the ground below us. I scream and cover my head as the hood of the bulldozer lands with a clang about thirty feet away and skids to a stop.

Wes leans over and puts his hands on his knees to catch his breath. "He okay?" he asks, gesturing to Quint with a flick of his head.

"He's alive, but ..." I drop my eyes to the glass sticking out of his neck and shake my head. "I don't know what to do."

God, I wish Mama were here. She would know. She was an ER nurse.

Was.

Now, she's dead.

Just like we're going to be if we don't get the hell out of here before that gas tank explodes.

I look around and realize that, with the light from the flames, I can actually tell where we are now. The sides of the highway are cluttered with all the cars and trucks that Quint and Lamar pushed out of our way, but the faded green exit sign on the side of the road says it all.

PRITCHARD PARK MALL

NEXT RIGHT

My eyes meet Wes's, and without saying a word, we get to work. He stashes the motorcycle in the woods, I drag the hood of the bulldozer over to make a stretcher for Quint, and Lamar shakes off his daze enough to stand and help carry his brother past the wreckage.

When we get to the exit ramp, Pritchard Park Mall sits at the bottom, shining in the moonlight like a worthless mountain of crumbling concrete. It's been rotting away ever since the last store closed up shop about ten years ago, but the land isn't valuable enough for anyone to even bother tearing it down.

"Fuck. Look at that place," Wes groans. He's holding one side of the makeshift stretcher while Lamar and I struggle with the other. "You sure about this?"

"I don't know where else to go," I huff, shifting my grip on the corner of the yellow hood. "We can't put Quint on the bike to take him home, we can't leave him here, and we can't sleep in the woods because the dogs will sniff out the food in our pack."

A howl rises over the sound of burning metal, pushing us to move faster.

"You okay, man?" Wes asks Lamar, changing the subject. He doesn't want to talk about what we might find inside this place any more than I do.

Lamar just nods, staring straight ahead. Quint's smart-ass little brother hasn't said a word since he came to, but at least he can walk. And follow directions. That's actually an improvement for him.

When we get to the bottom of the ramp, we find a chain-link fence circling the perimeter of the mall property. The sounds of gunshots, terrified screams, and revving engines fill the air—probably Pritchard Park rioters celebrating the fact that they survived April 23, but they obviously don't care about looting the mall.

They're smart enough to know there's nothing left to loot.

We walk along the fence until we find a spot that's been flattened. Then, we cross the parking lot and head toward what used to be the main entrance.

We pass a few cars with For Sale signs in their broken windows, kick a couple of hypodermic needles along the way, and eventually make it to a row of metal and glass doors. At least half of the windows have been broken out already, which makes the hair on the back of my neck stand up.

We're not the first ones here.

The bulldozer hood won't fit through the door, so we set it down on the sidewalk as carefully as we can.

"I'll go in first," Wes says, pulling the gun from his holster.

"I'm coming with you," I announce before glancing over at Lamar. "You stay with him."

But Lamar's not listening. He's staring at his big brother like he hung the moon.

And then fell from it.

"Don't you dare touch that glass," I add, pointing to Quint's neck. "He'll bleed out. Do you hear me?"

Lamar nods once but still doesn't look up.

When I turn back toward Wes, I expect him to argue with me about coming with him, but he doesn't. He simply offers his elbow for me to take and gives me a sad, exhausted, exquisite smile.

"No fight?" I ask, wrapping my hand around his tattooed bicep.

Wes kisses the top of my head. "No fight," he whispers. "I'm not letting you out of my sight."

Something in his words makes my cheeks flush. I should be afraid of walking into an abandoned mall with no electricity at night in the aftermath of The Apocalypse That Never Happened, but as Wes tucks me behind his back and pulls the broken door open, the only thing I feel is an overwhelming sense of belonging. I would follow this man to the ends of the earth, which, from the looks of it, might be right here at Pritchard Park Mall.

Wes guides us through the open door and eases it closed with the tiniest click. We tiptoe over the broken glass like professionals, and Wes leads the way with his gun stretched out in front of us.

The smell of a decade's worth of dust and mildew is overpowering. I have to clench my teeth and cover my nose with the sleeve of my hoodie to keep from coughing. The only source of light inside is the moon shining in through a few dirty skylights, but I came here so many times as a kid that I know the layout by heart.

At the end of this hall, there should be a fountain in the middle of a two-story atrium. I remember there being escalators behind it and elevators on the left—cool glass ones that I used to beg Mama to ride over and over and over. Branching out from the atrium, there are four hallways—this one leading to the main entrance, the north hallway that leads to the old food court, and two more on the left and right that lead to the big department stores that Mama always said we couldn't afford to shop at.

Even though I remember coming here as a kid, there's no sense of nostalgia. No warm familiarity. It's so dark and so vacant that I feel as though I'm walking on the moon and being told that it used to be Earth.

As the crumbling edges of the stone fountain come into view, the sound of voices in the distance has me pulling Wes to a stop.

I push up onto my tiptoes until my lips graze the shell of his ear. "Do you hear that?" I whisper. "It sounds like—"

"Freeze!" a voice shouts as the silhouette of a man holding a rifle appears from behind the fountain.

Instinctively, I hold my hands up and step in front of Wes. "Don't shoot!" I shout back. "Please! Our friends outside are hurt. We just need a place to spend the night."

"Rainbow?" His voice softens, and I recognize it instantly.

It's one I've heard say my name a thousand different times in a thousand different ways. It's one I never thought I'd hear again, and after I met Wes, never wanted to. It's the voice of the boy who left me behind.

"Carter?"

I thought April 24 was going to be a new beginning.

Turns out, it's just the beginning of the end.

Wes

CARTER.

His name on her lips hits my ears like a blaring, screaming alarm clock, waking me from the best dream of my life.

It all seemed so real. I can still feel the heat of her thighs around my waist and see the tears glistening in her big blue eyes when she told me she loved me. When she promised she'd never leave. And I believed her.

Like a fucking dumbass.

The impending apocalypse made people do crazy shit. Some burned entire cities to the ground. Some, like Rain's psychopathic dad, committed murder-suicides just to get it all over with. And me? I let myself believe the desperate ramblings of a lost, lovesick teenager.

But the four horsemen never came for us.

Reality did.

And from the looks of him, he's about six foot three.

Even though I feel like the world is tilting on its axis and there's an invisible knife twisting in my pancreas, I keep my cool as Reality jogs toward my girl.

No, not my girl. *His* girl.

I've done this so many times; it's almost second nature now. Standing in the Department of Child and Family Services while yet another foster parent gave me back. Standing against the lockers in my fuckteenth high school, acting like I didn't give a shit whether anyone talked to me or not. Standing behind the bar at work, watching whatever chick I was fucking at the time kiss her boyfriend goodbye in the parking lot.

Fold your arms across your chest. Keep your posture loose. Look bored. You are bored. People are so fucking boring. Yawn. Light a cigarette. Damn, no cigarettes.

Rain doesn't move as he approaches. She doesn't lift her arms for a hug, but that doesn't stop LeBron James from wrapping his four-foot-long arms around her and lifting her off the ground.

My teeth clench together, and my blood fucking boils as he goes to kiss her, but on the outside, I'm the picture of indifference.

Do what you want. I don't care.

You don't care.

Nobody fucking cares.

Rain turns her head before his lips can make contact and grunts, "Ugh! Carter, what are you doing? Put me down!"

He's just a shadow, but the whites of his eyes almost glow in the dark as they go wide and glance over at me.

I smirk and raise an eyebrow, but it's just for show. Kind of like Rain's performance right now. I'm not stupid enough to think this means she isn't going to go back to him. I know she is. I've seen this episode before.

"What am I doing?" His voice wavers as he sets her back on her feet. "I fucking missed you! I never thought I'd see you again. And you're *here*. You're ... *alive*."

Rain shoves him with both hands, and he takes a step backward, more out of shock that she pushed him than her actual strength.

"No thanks to you!" she screams. *Screams*. It knocks the dust off the rafters and scares a bird into flight.

I grip the handle of my gun and listen for footsteps. That pigeon can't be the only thing she just woke up.

"What was I supposed to do?" Carter reaches for her, and she shoves him again. "I had to go with my family!"

Yep. This is the part where she guilt-trips him for leaving ...

"One town over? I thought you were in Tennessee!"

"We were in a bad car accident and got stranded here." The giant huffs and drags a hand through his hair. "I'll tell you about it in the morning, okay? Come here."

"Stranded?" Rain swats his giant hands away. "You could *walk* back to Franklin Springs from here! It's twenty miles, max!"

"You know it's not safe to be on the roads! Especially with all the supplies we'd be carrying."

"You wanna talk to me about not being safe? You have no *idea* what I went through while you were gone!"

Aaaaand this is the part where she uses me to make him jealous ...

"I almost died! Wes, how many times did I almost die?" She keeps her back to me as Carter's head swivels in my direction.

Even though my throat is so tight that I can hardly breathe and I have to put my hands in my pockets to keep him from seeing that they're balled into fists, I manage to keep my voice unaffected when I say, "I dunno. Ten? Twelve? I lost count."

"Who the hell is *he*?" Carter thrusts a massive hand in my direction, and Rain looks at me over her shoulder.

I lock eyes with her, my feelings safely hidden behind a well-worn costume of confident apathy, and silently ask the same question.

Yeah, Rain. Who am I? Your substitute boyfriend? Your April 23 distraction? Your meal ticket? Chauffeur? Gravedigger and personal bodyguard? Just say it so that I can get the fuck out of here and go find something to break.

Rain takes a deep breath and smiles at me in a way that almost makes me think she means it. Her porcelain face lights up, illuminating the dust-thickened air around her, and her shiny blue doll eyes look wild and alive. I know that look. That's the look she gets before she does something stupid and impulsive.

"He's my fiancé." She beams.

Motherfucker.

My shoulders slump, and any doubt I had about her motives leaves me in a bitter, sharp sigh.

"Fiancé?" Carter jerks his head back as if he's been punched, but Rain isn't even facing him anymore.

She's walking toward me with a sway to her hips and a smirk on her beautiful fucking face.

"I just left a month ago! And besides, why the fuck would you get engaged if you thought we were gonna die yesterday?"

"I knew we weren't gonna die," Rain says, standing beside me and wrapping a delicate hand around my bicep. "Wes is a survivalist."

Carter throws his free hand in the air in exasperation as I look down at my girl. *His* girl.

Fine. I can play this game—the one where she pretends to care, and I pretend to believe her. I've been playing it my whole life. At least now, I know where I stand.

I thought April 24 was going to be a new beginning.

Turns out, it's just the same old shit but with no Wi-Fi.

"Hey, guys? We got trouble!" Lamar's voice coming from the mall entrance breaks up our happy little reunion.

We turn and run toward him as the sound of motorcycles revving and guns firing and people shouting builds outside.

"Shit," Carter hisses. "Bonys."

"What are Bonys?" Rain asks, but as Carter pushes the door open with one long arm, we're able to see for ourselves.

Dozens of motorcycle riders have blazed over the downed section of fence around the mall and are doing doughnuts and firing semiautomatic weapons into the air in the parking lot. Bullets leave their guns in orange bursts as they howl at the moon, matching the Day-Glo orange stripes painted on their clothes to look like skeleton bones.

"Oh my God! Is that Quint?" Carter slides his rifle around so that it's hanging down his back and leans over to get a better look at the guy we left outside.

In this light, I can see that Carter is no Franklin Springs redneck. The guy has brown skin and a mop of curly, dark hair, and he's wearing a fucking Twenty One Pilots T-shirt.

I think about the oversize Twenty One Pilots hoodie Rain was wearing when I first met her, and I have to resist the urge to kick his teeth in.

"We can't fit the hood through the door, so we're gonna have to lift him." Rain is in doctor mode, which is pretty much the only time she takes the lead on anything. "Wes, help me hold Quint's head and neck still, so the glass doesn't move. Lamar and Carter, you guys each take a leg. Come on! Now!"

Luckily, the doorway is shadowed by an awning, so the Bonys haven't noticed us yet. We do as Rain said and move Quint's lifeless body inside. The first empty store on the left has its metal gate down and locked, but the third shop is wide open. We shuffle inside and set Quint on the floor behind the checkout counter.

A faded sign on the wall announces that this place used to be called Savvi Formalwear.

Formalwear. In Pritchard Park. No fucking wonder this place went out of business.

Lamar kneels next to his brother and holds his hand while he feels for a pulse, and the sight of them knocks the air out of my lungs. I know that fucking feeling. I know what it's like to lose your only sibling. To find her quiet and cold in her crib. The moment I see Lily's blank, bluish face in my mind, I feel like I'm being choked. Strangled. I can't get out of there fast enough. I mumble something about guarding the door as I stumble backward out of the store.

Rain calls after me, asking for her first aid kit, so I tear her backpack off my shoulders and toss it onto the floor as I bolt.

I don't stop until I get to the entrance, bracing my forearms on the metal door handle and sucking in lungfuls of humid air through the broken glass.

Fuck, I hate it here.

The Bonys—or whatever they're called—are still tearing it up outside. I watch them in a jealous rage. Carter seemed afraid of them, but they look like they're having a good fucking time if you ask me. Not a care in the—

Suddenly, the entire mob takes off toward the road in front of the mall. It's so dark that I can't make out what triggered them to leave until their headlights close in on a dude riding a bicycle with a backpack on. Even from across the parking lot, I can see the terror on his face as they descend upon him like piranhas. His screams are loud enough to rise over the roar of their engines, and when they finally race off, there's nothing but some twisted metal and a fleshy lump in the road where a living, breathing man just was.

"Oh, good. They're gone." Rain's breathy voice sounds like heaven compared to the noises I just heard.

I tear my eyes away from the cadaver in the street and turn toward her, relieved to see that she's alone. I open my arms and hug her—I don't know why. I guess I just need to hold her before the next thing comes to try to take her away.

Rain hugs me back, and for a minute, we just stand there and take it all in.

"How's Quint?"

Rain sighs. "He's alive, but I don't know how long I can keep him that way. If I take the glass out, he'll lose too much blood, so I just cleaned him up and left it in. I'm hoping his body will push it out on its own. I heard that's a thing."

I force a reassuring smile and kiss the top of her head. "Yeah, that's a thing."

"Lamar's gonna stay with him tonight."

"Good."

"And Carter went back to his post by the fountain. He said he's on guard duty tonight."

"So, he's watching us right now."

Rain nods against my chest. "Probably."

I let her go and take a step back, searching her face for signs of sincerity. "And that whole thing about us being engaged …"

Rain blushes and drops her eyes. "I had a dream a few nights ago that we were lying in Old Man Crocker's field, and you made me a little engagement ring out of a blade of grass." Rain lifts her left hand and stares down at her empty finger. "It seemed so real, you know? Until you turned into a scarecrow and the four horsemen of the apocalypse came and set you on fire."

"You sure you weren't just trying to make your boyfriend jealous?"

Rain drops her hand and looks at me as if I just spat on her shoes. "Are you serious right now?"

"As a fucking heart attack."

"I said it because that's how I feel, Wes. I don't want to call you my *boyfriend*. I've had one of those, and it didn't feel like this." Rain casts a glance over her shoulder at the dark hallway stretching out behind her and the man-child sitting in the shadows beyond. "But considering that you didn't even fight for me back there, I'm guessing that you don't feel the same way."

I grab Rain by the jaw and pull her into the shadows of the storefront doorway right next to us. I hate the way her eyes go wide in fear, but it's taking all of my self-control not to scream in her face right now.

"Listen to me," I hiss through gritted teeth. "When I found you last night, I thought you were fucking dead." I spit the words out, remembering how heavy her lifeless body felt in my arms. How her hands dangled at her sides and her head fell back as I clutched her to my chest and cried against her cold, slack cheek. "For the first time in my life, I thought about killing myself. If I hadn't finally found your pulse, I was prepared to lie down right next to you and blow my own fucking brains out, so don't tell me how the fuck I feel."

Rain's mouth falls open in my palm as her eyebrows pull together in pain. "Wes …"

"I'll fight to keep you alive. I'll fight to keep you safe. But I will *never* fight to keep you, or anyone, from leaving me."

A tear slips from the corner of Rain's glassy eye and rolls down the edge of my index finger to her parted lips. Reaching out, she places one tiny hand over my heart, over the place where thirteen jagged tally marks tell the world how many foster homes I was kicked out of, how many times I wasn't good enough, how many times I fought to stay and was left behind anyway.

Then, she says the words that make me want to put my fist through the glass shop window beside her head, "You'll never have to."

I tilt her face up and kiss her salty, wet mouth until her breath becomes ragged and her hands begin to claw at my belt buckle. Carter can't see us—I made sure of that when I pulled her over here—so I know this isn't just for show. Rain actually believes the four little words she just whispered.

If only they were true.

Rain

"PLEEEEEASE!" I CRY, TUGGING on Mama's hand and leaning with my whole body toward the Hello Kitty store. "I promise I won't beg for nuthin'! I just wanna look. Real quick! Pleeeeease?"

"Rainbow, stop it," Mama snaps, looking around at all the other shoppers. "You're making a scene."

"But Tammy-Lynn got a Hello Kitty binder for her birthday!"

Mama's eyes get softer, and I know I got her. She never lets me get nuthin' at the mall unless it's my birthday, and it just so happens that I'm gonna be eight in exactly three days.

"One thing, okay? And you can't have it until your birthday."

"Yes, ma'am!"

This time, when I yank Mama's hand, she lets me pull her into the store, and it's like a Hello Kitty wonderland in there. Purses and T-shirts *and lamps and stuffed animals and bath mats and bedsheets and, "Oh my God, slap bracelets! Look, Mama! Look!"*

"One thing, Rainbow. And hurry up. We still have to get you some new shoes for school."

Shoes!

I run to the shoe wall and drool as rows and rows of Sanrio characters stare back at me from the sides of sneakers and sandals and even fuzzy little bedroom slippers. But one pair calls out to me. I grab the black low-top Converse with Badtz-Maru's cute little face right on top.

"I want these, Mama! Please?"

My mother scrunches her face up as she takes the shoebox out of my hands. "The grumpy penguin? Out of everything in this store, you want the black grumpy-penguin shoes?"

I bite my lip and nod all my nods.

Mama turns the box sideways in her hands and reads the description of my favorite Hello Kitty character out loud. "Bad Badtz-Maru is a mischievous little penguin who has dreams of becoming the king of everything one day. Although he's bossy and he has a bit of an attitude problem, Badtz is a loyal friend to Pandaba and Hana-Maru. When he's not getting into trouble, Badtz-Maru can be found collecting pictures of movie stars who play his favorite bad guys?" *Mama's voice goes up at the end like she's asking a question. "Rainbow!"*

"What, Mama? He's my favorite! Look how cute he is!"

"Cute? He's scowling."

I stick my finger out and stroke his frowny little canvas beak. "He just needs somebody to love him. That's all."

Mama sighs and slaps the lid on the box. "Fine, but only because it's your birthday."

We check out, and I don't even let the cash register lady put my shoes in a bag. I just hug the whole box to my chest and wait for the receipt to print. It prints and prints and gets longer and longer until it touches the floor.

I look up at the lady, but she's gone. Everybody's gone. The store is empty, and it smells bad, like the attic. Everywhere I look, the lights are off, and the shelves are empty. Even the shoe rack. The counter that was just shiny and white a second ago is now covered in dust so thick that I could write my name in it with my finger.

The receipt is still printing, so I follow it out the door and into the hallway. The benches are rusty now. The floor tiles are all cracked, and some even have grass growing in between them. And the sale banners that used to hang from the ceiling don't say Sale no more. They're all red with demon people riding black, smoke-breathing horses on them.

I don't like it here. I wanna go home.

I turn in circles, trying to find Mama, but she's gone too.

It's just me and Bad Badtz-Maru. Even though he's just on a pair of shoes, I know he'll protect me. He's going to be the king of everything one day.

I follow the receipt out the door and into the parking lot. It's empty now. More scary banners hang from the light posts, but I ain't afraid of them. I'm mad at them. They made everything go away. They made Mama go away. So I stomp over to a junky old car and climb up on top of it, all the way to the roof. Then, I reach up and pull one of those banners right down.

"There!" I yell, throwing it on the dirty ground. "See? You're not so—"

But I don't get to let all my words out before these real, real loud motorcycles drive up super-fast from all around me. The people driving them are dressed like skeletons, and some of their helmets have spikes on them.

I wonder for a minute if they're friends with the demon horse riders. I hug my shoebox tighter, hoping they won't be mad about me ripping down their friends' banner, but then they do something even worse than ripping the banners down. They start lighting them on fire!

I cheer and put my fist in the air like people do in the movies.

They hate the horsemen too! Maybe they'll help me. Maybe they know where everybody went. Maybe they can take me to my mama.

A few of the skeleton people see me and start driving their motorcycles in a circle around the car I'm on.

I smile. "See, Badtz," I whisper to my shoebox. "It's gonna be okay. We found some new friends."

There's a guy on the back of one of the motorcycles, and he's pouring something all over the car out of a big red jug. Some of it even splashes up onto my shoes.

"Hey!" I shout, taking a step back.

I wonder if maybe the guy driving will tell his friend that he's spilling his water, but he doesn't. Instead, he pulls to a stop right in front of me, flips open a fancy lighter—the silver kind that Daddy uses to light his cigarettes—and tosses it onto the hood of the car.

I wake up with a gasp, my eyes darting left and right, looking for signs of danger faster than my foggy brain can process what they're seeing.

I'm sitting on the ground inside the mall. My back is against Wes's chest. His arms are around my shoulders. In front of me, I can see the broken-out windows of the main entrance. It must have rained while we were asleep. There's a puddle creeping toward us from the door.

And one of my hiking boots is already soaked.

We're tucked inside of the same store entrance we hid in last night. The metal gate is down and locked, but I know without even peeking through the slats which shop it used to be. I can practically smell the Hello Kitty bath bombs and body sprays clustered around the checkout stand.

Wes tightens his grip around my body and grinds his teeth in his sleep. I want to let him hold me a little longer, but I can tell that whatever he's dreaming about is about as fun as being set on fire by Bonys.

"Wes." I tap his thigh, which is about all I can do with the death grip he has on me. "Wake up, babe. It's morning."

Wes swallows and yawns and rubs my upper arms with his hands as he comes to. "Hmm?"

"It's morning. We made it."

Wes shifts his weight and sits up straighter behind me. Then, he lets his forehead drop to my shoulder with a groan. "You woke me up for that?"

I laugh. "I thought you were having a nightmare. Did you see the horsemen?"

He grumbles something into my hoodie that sounds like a no.

"Really? Me either! I saw the banners, but the horsemen never came." I frown, thinking about how the Bonys were about to light me on fire, but at least it was something new. After spending a year dreaming about the four horsemen of the apocalypse killing everyone on April 23, getting burned alive by a deranged motorcycle gang feels like an improvement.

"Yeah, I saw the banners too." Wes yawns and lifts his head. "But then everybody turned into zombies and tried to eat us. I got to hack your boyfriend up with a machete though, so it wasn't all bad."

"Wes!" I turn sideways in his lap, ready to snap at him for using the B-word again, but the sight of him hits me like a ton of bricks.

His soft green eyes are rimmed with red. His jaw is peppered with stubble. His face is covered in dirt and ash, and the collar of his blue Hawaiian shirt has Quint's blood on it. The reality of what we've been through comes crashing down around me as I gaze into Wes's beautiful, battle-worn face.

It happened. All of it. The eighteen-wheeler explosion. The overdose. The house fire. The shoot-out at Fuckabee Foods. My parents …

Wes gets blurry as my eyes fill with tears. I squeeze them shut, trying to block out the images of my daddy in his armchair and my mama in her bed. Their faces … oh my God.

They're really gone, and the apocalypse never came to make it all go away.

I cover my mouth with the sleeves of my hoodie and look up at Wes. "What are we gonna do now?" My voice breaks along with the dam holding back my tears.

Wes pulls me against his chest and wraps his arms around me as an ocean of grief drags me under. "Don't you remember what I told you?" he asks, rocking my jerking, trembling body from side to side.

I burrow my face into the side of his neck and shake my head, gasping between sobs.

How can I remember what to do? I've never lost my entire family in one day before.

But Wes has.

"We say *fuck 'em* and survive anyway."

"Right." I nod, remembering his pep talk from two days ago.

"So, what do we need to survive today?"

I sniffle and lift my head. "You're asking *me*?"

"Yep. In order to say *fuck 'em* and survive anyway, the first thing you have to do is say *fuck 'em*, and the second thing you have to do is figure out what you need to survive. So, figure it out. What do we need?"

"Uh ..." I wipe the snot and tears from my face with my hoodie sleeve and sit up. "Food?"

"Good." Wes's tone is surprisingly not sarcastic. "Do we have any?"

"Um ..." I look around until I spot my backpack in the opposite corner of the entryway. "Yes. And water but not much."

"What else do we need?"

I look at the puddle inching closer to us. "A better place to sleep."

"Okay. What else?"

My eyes drop to the torn, bloodstained spot on Wes's sleeve. "You need to take your medicine. You need a new bandage too, but my hands aren't clean enough to do it."

"So, we'll add *find soap* to the list."

I nod again, surprised at how relieved I feel. Empowered almost.

"So we need supplies and shelter ..." he summarizes. "What else?"

"Hmm ..." I pull my eyebrows together and look around, hoping to find some clue in the dank, dusty, cobweb-covered hallway.

Wes clears his throat and taps the handle of the gun sticking out of his holster.

"My daddy's gun?"

"Self-defense." He smirks. "Supplies. Shelter. Self-defense. Every day, when you wake up, I want you to ask yourself what you need to survive that day, and then your job is to go find it."

"That's it?"

"That's it."

"Okay." I nod once, like a soldier accepting a mission. "So today, we need soap and water and a better place to sleep."

I like this—having a goal again. Taking direction. It feels like it did back when we were searching for the bomb shelter. When it was just me and Wes against the world. It was almost fun.

Wes smiles, but his tired green eyes don't even crease at the corners. There's a sadness in them that feels new. He usually looks so determined, so focused. Now he just looks ... resigned.

"See?" he says, letting his fake grin fall as two miserable mossy eyes bore through me. "You got this."

"*We* got this," I correct.

"Yeah." Wes swats me on the side of my butt and waits for me to climb off his lap. "Well, *we* have to take a piss, so ... time to get up."

We both stand, and I watch as he stretches and cracks his neck from side to side. He's gone—I can feel it. The fiery, passionate Wes that I was just beginning to get to know has become the Ice King again. Cold. Hard. Good at slipping through my fingers.

The air temperature seems to drop ten degrees as he breezes past me and over to the main entrance. When he doesn't hear anything outside, he pushes it open with his gun drawn and disappears into the foggy morning.

Wes said my job was to figure out what I need to survive and go get it.

But I already let it walk out the front door.

Wes

I'VE GOT MY DICK in one hand and my gun in the other as I piss on a dead bush outside of Pritchard Park Mall. No sign of the Bonys yet. I have a feeling they're not exactly morning people.

Fuck knows I'm not.

I zip my shit up, wishing like hell that I had a cigarette.

Rain's dad probably had a whole stash in their house somewhere.

I look past the parking lot, through the chain-link fence, and up the ramp to the overpass. The eighteen-wheeler wreckage is maybe a hundred feet before the exit, hidden from view by the woods—just like Rain's mom's perfectly good motorcycle. I feel the weight of the key in my pocket, calling to me.

Leave before you get left, it says.

I chew on my bottom lip. Then, I reach into my pocket and pull out the key.

Leave before you get left.

I look down at the keychain in my palm for the first time since grabbing it last night. Attached to the metal ring is a frayed strip of leather, knotted on both ends and strung with a dozen mismatched plastic beads. The ones in the middle spell out *I ♥ MOM.*

Leave, dumbass—

"Wes? Are you still out here?"

"Yeah." I spin around as Rain peeks her head out of one of the broken entrance doors.

Her big, round, puffy eyes lock on to me, and a giant smile spreads across her tear-streaked face. "One down, two to go."

I pull my eyebrows together, but before I can ask what she's talking about, Rain pushes the door open with her boot and holds her sparkling clean hands up so that I can see them.

"I found soap!"

I pocket the keychain and follow Rain back to the tux rental place where Quint and Lamar spent the night. Quint is still behind the counter, unconscious. His neck is bandaged, but the shard of glass is still there, poking out through the gauze. Lamar is sitting on the floor next to him with his back to the wall, and gauging by the bags under his eyes, I think he stayed up all night watching his brother breathe.

"The employee bathroom still has soap in the dispenser!" Rain chirps, pointing toward a hallway on the right side of the shop. "No running water though. I had to use some of the bottled stuff. Sit." She gestures toward the checkout counter.

I lean against it and toss a glance at Lamar. "You okay, man?"

He nods, but his eyes never leave his brother's face.

I wish I had something encouraging to say, like, *I'm sure he'll be okay,* or, *Rain will fix him up,* but the motherfucker hasn't moved a muscle since I pulled him out of that bulldozer last night. For all we know, he could be brain-dead.

Rain sets her backpack on the counter next to me and starts rummaging through it. She pulls out what's left of the antibiotics, a bottle of water, a first aid kit, and a handful of protein bars. I twist the cap off the orange pill bottle and shake a white tablet into my mouth as she peels back my bandage and takes a peek.

She exhales in relief and pulls it the rest of the way off. "It looks so much better, Wes."

I glance down at the mangled gash on my shoulder, laid open by that fucker's bullet, and hear Lamar suck his teeth behind us.

"Better than *what*? Got*damn*, that shit is *nasty*."

I cough out a bitter laugh. "You shoulda seen the other guy."

I picture those two gangbangers dropping to the ground in a spray of bullets and blood and broken glass. Then, I remember the horror I saw on Rain's face the moment she realized that she was the one who'd pulled the trigger.

It's the same look that's on her face now.

Shit.

I reach over and give her arm a squeeze. I forgot that she's not exactly happy about being a murderer.

Rain pretends not to notice as she places a new bandage on my upper arm, pressing the edges down with delicate fingers. Her touch makes all the other broken, hollowed-out places in me scream and beg for her attention too.

Goddamn, it hurts.

"Where's your daddy, Lamar?" Rain asks, changing the subject away from the shooting.

"Home." He punctuates his one-word sentence by spitting a wad of phlegm on the ground.

"He still alive?" Rain asks, trying to sound nonchalant, but I can hear her swallow that lump in her throat from here.

"I fuckin' hope not," Lamar grumbles.

She tucks her chin to her chest and begins shoving everything back into her backpack, probably to hide the fact that her hands are shaking.

Lamar opens his mouth like he's about to ask her about her own piece-of-shit dad, but then he shoots to his feet and sucks a deep breath in through his nose. "Y'all smell that?"

"Smell wha—" I inhale and can practically taste scrambled eggs on my tongue. "Holy shit."

"Breakfast time, bitches!" Lamar slaps the filthy counter and heads out the door.

I guess the only thing that can pull him away from his big brother is the promise of food that doesn't come out of a can. Typical teenage boy.

"What about Quint?" Rain asks, her eyes shifting from the open doorway over to me.

"He's not going anywhere." I sigh, tossing the protein bars back into Rain's backpack. "Come on. Let's go see what your boyfriend made you for breakfast."

Rain

NEITHER OF US SPEAKS as we walk through the atrium, following the smell of food.

I try to be tough, like Wes. I stand tall, take long steps to match his, but everything I look at reminds me of her. The escalators I used to beg Mama to let me ride over and over are just metal stairs now. The glass elevator with the big, glowing buttons I loved to press is stuck on the bottom floor—its only passengers a few Burger Palace wrappers and a plastic chair. The three-tier fountain that Mama and I used to throw pennies into is now full of weeds and baby pine trees. And, instead of Christmas music, all I hear is broken tiles clattering under our boots and the sound of voices coming from the direction of the food court.

Everything hurts. My eyes burn. My chest aches. My family is gone. The world I knew is gone. And all I want to do is curl up in that plastic chair in that broken elevator and cry myself to death.

But I know Wes won't let me, so I keep going. I keep trying to breathe. I keep trying to remember what was on my survival to-do list. But mostly, I keep trying to figure out what I can do to get Wes back. *My* Wes. Not this detached tough-guy version.

As we pass through the atrium and approach the food court, I wish the walk had been longer. I'm not ready for this.

There are people everywhere. I was expecting Carter and his family and maybe a few other stragglers who had made their way here after getting stopped by the wreck, but this is at least twenty people, talking and laughing and sitting at tables that have been clustered into small groups. The left and right sides of the food court are lined with fast-food counters. The back wall has an exit that's been barricaded shut with tables. The merry-go-round in the corner is still there, but it's tilted to one side and blanketed in cobwebs. And in the center, Carter's dad is standing next to a flaming barrel with a metal grate on top, cooking something in a cast iron skillet.

"Mr. Renshaw!" I cry, bounding over to the human teddy bear.

Carter's dad looks like a lumberjack Santa Claus—all beard and belly—and he always gives the best hugs.

His face lights up when he sees me, which is half a second before I tackle him and burst into tears.

"Come on now …" He chuckles, his deep voice vibrating against my cheek. "I ain't that ugly, am I?"

"Rainbow? Oh my goodness, child." Mrs. Renshaw's voice is husky and warm as she walks up and smooths her hand over my shorter hair.

She's tall and heavyset, like Carter's dad, but that's where their similarities end. Mrs. Renshaw is a no-nonsense black woman who was an assistant principal at our school before the world fell apart. She used to have a sleek, shoulder-length bob, like a TV reporter, but now her hair is cropped in a super-short Afro, probably due to the lack of hair salons in the Pritchard Park Mall.

"Shh …" she coos. "We should be celebratin', not cryin'. It's April 24. Come on now. Let's get you somethin' to eat. You must be starved."

When Carter's mom goes to fix me a plate of scrambled eggs from the skillet, I notice Wes standing a few feet away. The way he's watching us, with those intense eyes and that bored expression, makes me cry even harder. Because as much as I love Carter's parents, it's Wes's arms I want to be wrapped in right now. It's his punishing kisses and powerful hands that could make this pain go away. It's his love that could replace what I've lost.

But he's gone too.

Just like in my dream, Wes is nothing more than a scarecrow now, waiting to be burned.

Once I catch my breath, Mrs. Renshaw sits us down at a table nearby. The fake wooden surface is cleaner than anything I've seen in the mall so far, just like the metal chairs surrounding it. They obviously get some use. Carter and Lamar are at the table next to us along with Sophie, Carter's ten-year-old sister. She rushes over and hugs me from behind. Her dark corkscrew curls are wild, same as the other boy who's watching me right now.

Carter's eyes are a warm brown, but his stare is cold and questioning as it flicks from me to Wes.

"We haven't been properly introduced," Mrs. Renshaw says, extending her hand across the table to Wes.

"Oh, sorry." I pull my gaze from Carter to his mother. "Mrs. Renshaw, this is Wes. Wes, this is Carter's mom and dad." I reach up and tug on one of the curls smooshed against the side of my face. "And this little brat is Sophie."

"Hi!" Sophie giggles and squeezes me one more time before taking her seat by her brother.

"Wes and Rainbow here are *engaged*," Carter announces to the group, his voice oozing sarcasm.

Everyone's eyes fall on me as I squirm in my seat and stare at my untouched plate of food.

"Engaged?" Carter's mom echoes, dropping her fork.

I can't even speak. My cheeks burn with embarrassment and rage and shame as people who thought I would one day be their daughter-in-law stare at me like I have two heads.

"Yep," Carter sneers, looking at me like a cat that just found a rubber mouse. "Why don't you tell us how he popped the big question, Rainbow? Or did *you* ask *him*?"

"Carter!" his mother hisses in warning. "Stop it."

I go to push my chair out, ready to run away and hide until my face goes back to its regular color, but Wes's arm clamps around my shoulders before I can take off. He still feels cool and distant, but his icy aura is soothing now, like a balm.

"Can I tell the story, sweetheart?" Wes's voice is steady and strong, like his fingers as they stroke my upper arm.

I nod and slump against his side, wishing I could disappear altogether.

"So, after *you* left Rain in Franklin Springs with her deranged father ... he took a shotgun to her mom's face while she was asleep, blasted a hole in Rain's bed—which he didn't know was empty at the time—and then redecorated the living room with his own brains."

I wince and cover my face with my hoodie sleeves as everyone in the food court gasps and goes silent.

"I met her ... I don't know ... was it the next day, baby?"

I nod against his chest, too stunned to cry and too mortified to look up.

"When I found her, she was high as a kite, getting her ass kicked in the middle of Burger Palace over a bottle of painkillers."

"Oh, Rainbow. I'm so—"

"She goes by Rain now, and I'm not finished," Wes snaps, cutting off Carter's mother. "Since you guys left, she lost her parents, got shot at, got trapped in a house fire, tried to overdose, and ... what else, honey? Oh yeah, she almost got blown up in an eighteen-wheeler explosion last night. So, if

34

you're asking how we got *engaged* instead of why she's crying and looks like she's been through a war zone, you never fucking cared about her in the first place."

I wait for Carter's mom to slap him across the face, but all I hear is a single slow clap coming from the group of tables at the back of the food court. I open one eye and see a girl about my age, maybe younger, walking toward us with the swagger of a gangster. She looks like she might have had green hair at one point, but it's faded to the color of decaying leaves and is twisted into messy dreadlocks. Her rounded nose has a hoop through it, and her baggy black T-shirt and pants look like they came from the men's big and tall section at Walmart.

Everyone in the food court cowers as she passes.

"That's the most fun we've had around here since the internet went down." She twists her full lips into a smirk, still clapping at a painfully slow rate.

Wes's grip around my shoulders loosens, and his energy goes cool again.

"What's your name, *Hawaii Five-0*?" Her hazel eyes are the same color as her yellowish-greenish-brownish hair. They cut over to me once and darken before darting back over to the man next to me.

"Wes," he says flatly.

"Well, *Wes*, welcome to my kingdom." She spreads her arms and glances around the food court. "I'm Q. That stands for queen, 'cause I'm the muhfuckin' monarch up in here. Me and my crew been runnin' this place goin' on three years now. You and y'all other stray cats"—she flicks her fingernails at the rest of us sitting around the table—"are guests in my castle. That means y'all gon' have to pull y'all's weight, or you gon' get put out." Her angular eyebrows shoot up in warning as she points toward the barricaded exit.

"Ya boy Carter here"—she points a lazy finger at my ex—"is on patrol duty. *Duck Dynasty* over here hunts birds and deer and shit from up on the roof. And mama bear"—she points to Mrs. Renshaw—"cooks it all up real nice. But y'all ..." Q taps her fingertips to her lips as her eyes roam from Wes to me to Lamar. Then, she snaps her fingers. "Y'all gon' be my scouts."

"Scouts?" Wes's body language is relaxed, but his tone is challenging.

"That's right. We're runnin' low on shit now that all y'all strays are up in here. *Somebody* got to do some shoppin'."

"I can't leave," I blurt out. "Please. Let me do something else. We have a hurt friend, and somebody has to stay here to take care of him."

Q eyes me suspiciously. "You good at shit like that?"

"Like what?"

"Like nurse-type shit."

I sit up and nod. "My mom is … *was* … an ER nurse. She taught me a lot."

Q snaps again and points one long fingernail right between my eyes. "Good. You gon' be my medic. And you can start with that one." She swings her finger from my face to Mr. Renshaw's.

I glance at Mr. Renshaw and watch the color drain out of his rosy cheeks.

"Don't let me down now." Q cackles as she sashays back to her table, full of other rough-looking, gun-toting, unwashed teens. "I'd hate to have to feed y'all to the Bonys."

They're runaways, I realize.

We're all just strays and runaways.

Turning to Carter's dad, who hasn't spoken a word since we sat down, I ask, "Why do you need a medic, Mr. Renshaw?"

He gives me a sad smile. "That ain't important right now. What's important is that you know how sorry we are about your folks, Rainbo—I mean, Rain." Carter's grizzly bear of a dad looks at Wes, remembering what he said about my name, and gives him a solemn nod.

Mrs. Renshaw reaches across the table and squeezes my hand. "I am so sorry, baby girl." Her dark brown eyes glisten as they bore into mine. "I knew we shoulda taken you with us—you and your mama. I won't ever forgive myself for that, but at least we're all together now."

Lamar and Sophie both get up to hug me and give their condolences, but my attention is focused solely on Carter. The boy I grew up with. The boy I gave all my firsts to. The *man* who should be consoling me right now. But instead, he's just staring at me like he doesn't know what to say.

"Rainbow ..." he finally mutters.

"Rain," I snap back.

His honey-colored eyes fill with remorse, and for a second, I regret being so mean. That face ... I was in love with that face for as long as I can remember. I know every angle. Every expression and smile and dimple. It kills me to see him hurting. I want to curl up in his lap and let him wrap his long arms around me like he used to ...

But then I remember overhearing Kimmy Middleton say she made out with him senior year, and suddenly, I don't feel so bad anymore.

"Hey, Carter, remember Kimmy?" I watch the guilt crawl across his handsome face, and it's all the validation I need. "She burned your house down."

"What?" Mrs. Renshaw screeches. "Our house?"

Carter's eyes go wide and dart from me to his parents.

Sophie starts to cry.

Mr. Renshaw stands up, slams his chair in, and stomps away with a definite limp.

"What happened to him?" I ask, desperately wanting to change the subject after the bomb I just dropped on them. "Why does he need a medic?"

Mrs. Renshaw shakes her head and looks over her shoulder as her husband hobbles toward the atrium. "We got in a bad accident on our way out of town. As soon as we left for Tennessee, it was obvious that everybody on the highway was under the influence of something. People were speedin' and weavin' all over the road. We had only made it to Pritchard Park when a car up ahead of us pulled in front of a tractor-trailer and made it jackknife right in the middle of the road. It ended up rolling about three times and blocking the entire highway. There was a huge pileup, and we were caught right in the middle of it."

"Oh my God." I cover my mouth with the sleeve of my hoodie. "That pileup is why we're here too. We couldn't get around it, and when we tried ..." My voice trails off as I glance over at Lamar.

He's staring blankly in the direction of the tuxedo shop, like he can see his brother from here.

Mrs. Renshaw is looking at her children the same way. "Sophie and Carter were okay—thank God. But Jimbo ..." She shakes her head. "His leg was crushed in the accident, and he won't let anybody look at it. I'm afraid it's bad."

"So that's why you guys didn't come home?" I ask. "Because he couldn't walk that far?"

Mrs. Renshaw nods.

"Plus, the dogs and Bonys," Carter adds, staring at the table like a kid in the principal's office. "We never would have made it."

"So we decided to stay here. We had enough food and supplies in the car to last us this long, and Q has been gracious about sharing the drinking water from their rain barrels with us."

Q.

I glance over at the runaways' table and catch her watching us.

No. Not *us.*

Wes.

"When we woke up this morning and the apocalypse hadn't happened, I thought ..." Mrs. Renshaw's chin buckles. "I thought maybe things would go back to normal. Maybe we could go back home."

Carter's mom tries to hold it together, but as soon as she looks over at Sophie, her face crumples like a paper towel. I've never seen Mrs. Renshaw cry before, and knowing that my words made her do it makes me want to throw up. I was so cruel. My mama had taught me better than that. I was trying to hurt Carter on purpose, and this is what I get.

Carter, Sophie, and I all jump up at the same time to comfort her. Sophie kneels at her side and clasps her hand while Carter and I end up standing on either side of her, squeezing her shoulders and rubbing her back.

"I'm so sorry," I mutter, speaking to Mrs. Renshaw but finding my eyes drifting up to Carter's.

"Me too." His deep voice vibrates around me, taking me to a million different places at once.

I know what his voice sounds like when he's sleepy, when he's sick, when he's lying, when he wants me to take my clothes off, when he's angry, when he's frustrated, and when he's playing the part of Mr. Popular. I know what it sounded like when he was six years old and lost his two front teeth at the same time. And now, I know what it sounds like when he's just plain lost.

"You can have my house, Mrs. Renshaw," I say, tearing my eyes away from her son. "I'm never going back there again."

Wes

"WES, WAIT!" RAIN CALLS out, but I just keep walking.

I'd rather give myself a root canal than sit around for another second of this precious little family reunion.

"Rainbow!" Carter yells after her.

I turn around at the sound of his voice, only because I want to watch her choose him. *Them.* I need to see it. I need to feel the twist of the knife because I know that's the only fucking way I'll be able to let her go.

"Sorry. I meant, *Rain* ..." Carter has this bullshit, pitiful puppy-dog look on his pretty-boy face, and I want to put my fucking fist through it. "Can we go somewhere and talk? Please?" He pulls his eyebrows up so high that they disappear behind his mop of curly black hair. Then, he bites his bottom lip.

Motherfucker. I know that look. I invented that fucking look.

"Not right now, Carter," Rain says, picking up her untouched plate of eggs. "I have to go check on Quint."

Not right now? How about not fucking ever?

I feel my muscles tense and my teeth grind together as I glare at the piece of shit in the Twenty One Pilots T-shirt, but by the time his eyes land back on me, I'm loose as a motherfucking goose. I roll my neck and stick my hands in my pockets like I'm waiting in line at the DMV, not thinking of all the ways I could crack his skull open.

Rain turns and walks toward me, her face flushing when she realizes I stopped to watch their little exchange, but I keep my face slack and my posture relaxed.

You're not mad. You're bored. Bored, bored, bored.

Everybody knows how this show is gonna end. Rain becomes a Renshaw. She gets her happy little family back. They have two-point-five kids who can dunk from the foul line and don't even need therapy. The. Fucking. End.

I wait for her to catch up. Only a jealous, bitter asshole would turn his back and keep walking right now, and I'm not jealous.

Nope. I'm just so fucking bored.

Rain's face looks tortured as she approaches, and I feel the fire inside me die down. Her right cheek still has three pink claw marks on it from when she got attacked at Burger Palace. Her lips are chapped. Her hair is matted. And her big, round eyes look like two empty swimming pools now.

Drained.

Dull.

Desperate.

I hate how badly I want to be the one to fill them back up.

A moment before Rain closes the distance between us, gasps and shrieks and, "Oh my God!"s fill the food court. I look past her and see that every digital monitor behind every fast-food counter is on and glowing red.

"Wes?" Rain's voice is barely a whisper as she comes to stand beside me. "What's going on?"

I watch as the black silhouette of a hooded horseman holding a scythe flashes on-screen for less than a second.

"Did you see that?"

I nod.

Another one flashes—this time, the horseman with the sword. Then, another and another. Faster and faster, their images appear and disappear until the screens are just pulsating black-and-red pools.

People scream.

Sophie dives for her mother's arms.

And Rain grips my bicep so hard that her nails break the skin.

"Maybe this is just the nightmare," I say in a half-assed attempt to make her feel better.

"It's not, Wes. It's real."

"None of this is real, remember? It's all just a hoax."

"Citizens," a female voice with a French accent booms through the speakers, drawing my attention back to the screens.

The face of a middle-aged woman with mousy-brown hair, sharp features, and dark red lipstick fills the left side of the screen while the word *citizens* is written in at least twelve different languages on the right side.

"My name is Dr. Marguerite Chapelle. I am the director of the World Health Alliance. If you are seeing this broadcast, congratulations. You are now part of a stronger, healthier, more self-sufficient human race."

Rain and I look at each other as dread slithers across her face and into my veins.

The camera zooms out, and Dr. Chapelle is sitting at a sleek white table with an older man on either side of her. Behind them, on risers, are at least eighty other assholes, all wearing suits that probably cost more than the mortgage payments on their Malibu summer homes.

The smug bastard front and center is our fucking president.

"For the past year, the World Health Alliance has been working in conjunction with the United Nations"—she gestures to the world leaders standing behind her—"to implement a solution to the global population crisis. A *correction*, if you will. We call this correction Operation April 23."

"Wes, what is she talking about?" Rain whispers, gripping my arm tighter.

"Approximately three years ago, our top researchers discovered that, at the rate that our population was growing, Earth's natural and economic resources would be depleted in less than a decade. To put it bluntly, human beings were facing extinction, and the cause was simple—our species had abandoned the law of natural selection."

The camera pans to the man on her left, a skinny guy with a haircut like Hitler's. The caption below his face says, *Dr. Henri Weiss, World Health Alliance Researcher.* "Every s-species on the planet is s-subject to the law of natural selection," he says, tugging at his collar and taking a sip from his glass of water. His accent sounds German, and he looks like he's about to shit himself. "It is the very f-foundation of evolution. Since the dawn of living organisms, the weaker, more infirm members of the s-s-species die off, and the strongest, most intelligent, most well-adapted members live the longest and procreate the most. This p-process promotes the survival of the species by ensuring that each g-g-generation inherits only the most adaptive genetic traits and by p-p-preventing resources from being depleted by nonproductive s-s-s-subgroups."

The camera slides back to the French bitch. "Over the past century, human beings have become the first species to ever circumvent the law of natural selection. Through advances in technology and lavish government programs, we have been actively prolonging the lives of our weakest, most disabled, and most dependent members of society to the great detriment of our entire species."

She gestures to President Dickhead standing behind her.

"The American government, for example, spends over one trillion dollars each year housing, feeding, and caring for its disabled, incarcerated, and unemployed citizens—citizens who contribute nothing in return. As a result, the World Health Alliance calculated last January that the number of disabled and nonproductive members of our species outnumbered able-bodied, productive members for the first time in the history of any species. Immediate action had to be taken."

The camera cuts to the man on her right who looks a little like Mr. Miyagi from *The Karate Kid*. The caption below his name reads, *Dr. Hiro Matsuda, World Health Alliance Researcher*. "We needed a way to thin the herd, so to speak, while ensuring that the strongest, healthiest, most intelligent members of our species would survive. Engineering a super virus or inciting a world war would have been ... counterproductive ... due to the loss of healthy, able-bodied citizens that would have resulted. Therefore, my team and I came up with a plan to introduce a global stressor so intense that it would trigger our least resilient citizens to behave in self-destructive ways while simultaneously encouraging our most resilient citizens to become even stronger and more self-reliant."

The images of the horsemen appear again, eliciting gasps from the audience, but this time, they're presented as icons at the bottom of the screen.

"The Four Horsemen of the Apocalypse, the Grim Reaper, Death—these archetypes have appeared in almost every society throughout history. By planting these iconic images in every digital media source worldwide—paired with a single date: April 23—we were able to tap directly into the collective human subconscious and plant the idea of an impending doomsday."

"Oh my God, Wes," Rain whispers, looking up at me like a child who just found out that the Easter Bunny wasn't real. "Those images you found in my phone—you were right."

"Worldwide subliminal messaging." I shake my head.

Only it wasn't at the hands of some evil corporation or a band of sniveling computer hackers on a power trip, like I thought. It was worse.

It was our own fucking government.

"We all owe Dr. Matsuda, his team, and our world leaders a debt of gratitude." The French bitch grins. "Operation April 23 was a brilliant success. Our researchers estimate that our global population has been decreased by as much as twenty-seven percent with most of the relief coming from our nonproductive subgroups."

"What does that even mean?" Rain whispers.

"It means that most of the people who died because of the April 23 hoax were either crazy, sick, poor, or old."

I watch Rain's face go pale, and I wish I could take it back. *Shit.*

I pull her against my chest and press my lips to the top of her head. I don't even know what to say. All I can do is stand here and hold her while the government tells her they're happy that her parents are dead.

"In an effort to protect the law of natural selection going forward and to ensure that our population never again faces extinction due to our irresponsible allocation of resources to the weakest, most dependent members of society, all social services and subsidies are to be discontinued. Life support measures are to be discontinued. Government-provided emergency services are to be discontinued, and all incarcerated members of society will be released."

The entire food court erupts in outraged shouts and hushed murmurs as people try to process what the fuck this lady just said.

"You are encouraged to resume your daily lives. Power, water, and cell service have been restored, and the images you just saw have been removed from all digital media. Go back to work. Provide for your families. Protect yourself and your community. Your government will no longer do these things for you. And should you see evidence of a person or group of persons defying the laws of natural selection, you are required to dial 55555 on any cellular device to report the misconduct. Agents from your area will be dispatched immediately to detain the suspect. The future of our species depends on your cooperation. Good luck, and may the fittest survive."

The monitors go black as the reality of our situation slowly begins to take hold.

It was all just a fucking hoax.

They invaded our dreams.

They terrorized us from the inside out.

They drove us insane and watched while we self-destructed.

Then they smiled and said it was for our own good.

I wish I could say I was surprised, but after everything I've been through, this just feels like a regular Tuesday. Get shit on. Get beat down. Get told it's your fault. Then, get kicked to the curb with everything you own in a trash bag over your shoulder.

Yep, that sounds about right.

The only family in the room is clinging to one another for support. Offering comfort. Rationalizing that everything is going to be okay. Encouraging each other to trust in our leaders and do as they say.

Meanwhile, the homeless kids in the back of the room are jumping up and down, cheering and waving their guns in the air, while Q stands on a table shouting, "It's the wild, wild west, muhfuckas! Pew, pew, pew!"

The way Rain is wrapped around me, it's obvious which group she belongs in.

It's also obvious that I don't belong here at all.

Rain

"DUDE, THIS PLACE HASN'T had power in, like, forever, right? How in the hell did they make the TVs come on?" Lamar asks from his perch on the counter, his heels banging into the cabinets below with every swing of his restless legs.

Wes shrugs. "I dunno, man. Maybe they flipped the entire power grid on just for the broadcast?"

I'm only half-listening to their conversation. The rest of me is busy staring at the unconscious boy behind the counter. The one with the glass shard sticking out of a bloody bandage on the side of his neck. The one I'm supposed to fix somehow.

The one I'm *going* to fix somehow.

"Rain?" Wes asks.

"Huh?" I reply without taking my eyes off of Quint.

"You okay? You haven't said a word since the announcement."

"*The announcement*," I mutter, turning to face Wes. "Is that what we're gonna call it from now on? Like the way everybody called the apocalypse *April 23* 'cause it sounded nicer?"

Wes chews on his bottom lip like he does when he's trying to figure something out.

When he's trying to figure *me* out.

"I know that was a lot to process, okay? *I know*. But I need you to stay focused. Don't freak out on me."

"I'm not freaking out."

Wes tosses a doubtful glance at Lamar.

"I'm not. Maybe I just don't feel like talking about the fact that the government just publicly patted themselves on the back for makin' my dad try to kill his whole family."

Wes exhales hard through his nose and nods. "Yeah, I get that."

"I know he was *nonproductive*. He was depressed … unemployed, paranoid, mean as a snake, addicted to everything he could get his hands on … but what about *her*?" The prickly heat of anger in my flushed face fades as my throat tightens with emotion. "She was so good, Wes." I picture my mama's beautiful, frazzled, selfless face, and I want to cry. She was the most productive member of society I'd ever met. There are so many things I want to say, so many feelings I haven't expressed yet, but they're all too damn painful, so I cover my mouth with the sleeves of my sweatshirt and hold them all in.

I stare at Wes's lips, hoping the words coming out of his mouth will help take my mind off the ones lodged in my throat.

"I know. But we can't change what happened. All we can do is say *fuck 'em* and survive anyway, right? So, how are we gonna survive today? Do you remember your list?"

I swallow down all the things left unsaid and force myself to answer him.

"I … I was supposed to find soap, water, and shelter." I take a deep breath and straighten my back. "I already found soap, and Mrs. Renshaw said that Q has water barrels, so that only leaves shelter."

The lips I'm staring at widen and part, revealing Wes's dazzling smile. I don't get to see it often, but when I do, it warms my skin like the sun, seeping into my pores and filling me with pride.

I feel my own lips curve upward, mirroring his. I did something right.

"That's my girl," Wes says with that grinning mouth, but the moment the words pass over his upturned lips, his smile deflates like a popped balloon. He didn't like the way they tasted. This new, detached Wes didn't like calling me *his* girl.

So my lips fall flat too.

We stand there for a minute—me staring at his serious mouth and him staring at mine—until Wes finally takes a step back and gestures with his hand toward the door. "Let's go find you some shelter."

You.

"Let's go find you *some shelter."*

I want to take his arm as I make the short trip across the store, but I'm afraid I'll prick my finger on the barbed-wire fence he's building between us.

I don't know what's going on with Wes, but he's eerily quiet as we walk down the hallway. I yank on the metal gates and locked doors of every storefront we pass, but he just follows four feet behind me with his arms folded across his chest.

The distance between us feels like it's doubling with every step I take.

I turn right at the fountain and head down the hallway, angry tears stinging my eyes.

Hope momentarily chases them away when I spot an old shoe store up ahead with the gate raised. I poke my head inside and peek over the empty chest-high shelves. The vinyl benches that were once used to try on shoes have been clustered together in the center of the store and arranged like living room furniture. Carter's dad is sitting on one with his head bowed as Carter's mom and sister stand with their backs to me, probably telling him all about *the announcement.*

"Never mind," I whisper, slinking backward out of the store. "This one's taken."

When I turn to continue my walk, I find Wes waiting for me with his back against the graffiti-covered wall outside the shoe store. His Hawaiian shirt is open, revealing his bloodstained white tank top and the hint of a gun holster underneath. His head is tilted back, staring up at one of the skylights as if it were clear enough to actually see through, and his profile is the picture of perfection. The sight of him takes my breath away, replacing it with a hollow, empty ache in my chest.

He looks exactly like the man I fell in love with a few days ago. The one who rescued me from an angry mob, got shot for me, ran back into a burning building to find me, and buried my parents' bodies just to help take away my pain. He looks like the man who refused to let me go when everybody else had left me behind.

But he did let me go. He must have.

Because this guy sure as hell ain't him.

"You're not even helping me look," I snap, stomping past his cool exterior without stopping.

"You're right." Wes's voice is infuriatingly calm as he pushes off the wall.

"Is this some kind of test?" I hiss, rattling the next gate a little harder. "I have to do everything on my own from now on, is that it?"

"Nope," Wes says from somewhere behind me. "I'm not helping 'cause I'm not staying here."

"What?" I turn to face him, blood thumping in my ears. "Why not?"

That damn eyebrow goes up again. "Hmm. Maybe 'cause there's no running water. No electricity. Maybe I don't feel like being the errand boy for a group of crazy-ass, gun-toting homeless kids. Or, I don't know, maybe I don't wanna live down the hall from your fucking ex and his little Norman Rockwell family."

"What do you want me to do, Wes?" I turn my back on him and stomp toward the next storefront.

"Leave. With me. Right now. We can find a new place. One with water and power and doors that lock and walls that don't have black fucking mold growing on them."

I sigh, letting my hand linger on the rusty metal. "I can't leave Quint here. You know that."

"So, we'll take him with us. We could drive the Ninja back to town, gas up your dad's truck, and then come back and get him."

"What about Lamar?" My voice takes on a shrill tone as a strange sense of panic washes over me.

"He could ride in the back with Quint."

I turn and walk past the next entrance without stopping. The gate is up, but it's obvious somebody's been living in there for a while now. Maybe a few somebodies. Clothes and mattresses and beer cans and random, mismatched patio chairs are strewed around like confetti.

"What about Mr. Renshaw?" I ask, quickening my pace. "He's hurt too."

"You can make all the excuses you want. I know the real reason you don't want to leave."

"Oh, yeah? What's that?"

Because I'm too scared. Because I'm too sad. Because no one is trying to rape or rob me in here. Because nothing in here reminds me of home.

When Wes doesn't say anything, I turn to find him watching me with that emotionless expression on his filthy, beautiful face.

"You think I want to stay because of *him*?" I snap.

Wes raises one eyebrow as he nonchalantly chews on the inside corner of his mouth.

"Oh my God. I have friends here, Wes. I have a—"

"*Family*?" His tone is smooth as ice, but his eyes are hard and accusing.

"No ... a *purpose*. I can help people here. I feel safe in here. Out there ..." I shake my head, thinking about what's waiting beyond those doors. "Out there, it's nothing but Bonys and bad memories."

Wes opens his mouth to reply as I yank on the next metal gate. I brace myself for the impact of his words, but instead, my ears are assaulted by the sound of squealing gears when the gate jerks to life in my hands.

The rusty metal squeaks and shimmies as it rolls up to the ceiling, revealing the hollowed-out interior of an old Barnes & Noble bookstore.

My mouth falls open as I step inside. "Oh my God. This used to be my favorite place in the whole mall."

It's dark inside, but there's enough light from the skylights in the hallway to see my way around. The checkout stands are to the left of the entrance, right where I remember. The coffee shop, or what's left of it, is to the right. There are rows and rows of empty shelves in the center of the store and dust-covered tables lining the main aisle.

"I remember Mama bringing me here for story time when I was a kid," I continue, talking more to myself than to Wes. "They had a train set right back there, and these little stools that looked like tree trunks, and"—I gasp as my eyes climb up a wooden ladder in the far-left corner of the store, leading up the trunk of a cutout, cloud-shaped oak tree—"a tree house!"

I sprint down the main aisle, looking for signs of life between every row of shelves. When I don't find anything except for trash, standing water, and the occasional forgotten book, I head over to the children's area.

Please don't let anyone be up there. Please, God. Please let me have this one thing ...

I reach out with a hopeful hand to grasp the ladder, but Wes beats me to it. Taking the rungs two at a time, he climbs to the top and shines his pocket flashlight into the wooden shelter. Then, without a word, he clicks it off and hops back down, landing before me with a graceful thud.

"Well?"

"Well, what?" His face is unreadable, but the air around him is charged.

"Any runaways living up there?"

"Nope." Wes props his elbow on the ladder and leans over me, causing me to tilt my head back to make eye contact. "It's all yours."

"You mean, ours," I whisper, frozen to the spot by his icy stare.

Wes shakes his head. Slowly.

Panic shoots through my veins as I realize what he's saying.

"Don't go." I shake my own head, much faster, as sudden, uncontrollable tears blur my vision. "Please. Please stay here with me. I can't do this without you, Wes."

"Yes, you can."

"I don't want to!"

I step up onto the bottom rung of the ladder and place my hands on Wes's shoulders, so that we're eye-to-eye. "Remember yesterday? We were just like this. I was on the ladder of my tree house, and you were on the ground, and the sun was setting over there"—I point one hand in the direction of the hazy, sunlit entrance—"and I told you I loved you, and you said you loved me too."

"You thought the world was about to end." Wes's tone is condescending and doubtful, but his hands on my waist are begging me to make him believe.

"So did you."

"I meant what I said."

"So did I, Wes. I still do."

Seconds go by as I let that sink in. Wes doesn't say a word. He doesn't move a muscle, but his heart is beating so hard that I can feel the air vibrating off his chest in sonic waves. His hands tighten around my middle, and his nostrils flare as he sucks in silent breaths.

I can almost hear the sound of cracking ice.

I force a smile even though I'm terrified and bring one hand up to stroke his rough cheek. "Hey … if I'm not allowed to freak out, then you're not allowed to either."

Wes nods his head maybe a fraction of an inch. It's so subtle that I almost miss it, but in that whisper of movement, he lets me see the real him. The one who is panicking just as badly as I am.

"Look around, baby. It's still just you and me … and a tree house." I smile and gesture above my head. "Carter being here doesn't change anything. I don't want to stay because of him. I know that's what you think, but you're wrong. I want *you*. I love *you*. Don't you see that?"

Wes swallows the distance between us in a single step and crashes his lips against mine. When he presses my back against the ladder and invades my mouth with his tongue, I taste his relief. When he lifts my thigh over his hip and rocks against me, I feel his desperation. And when his hand slides up the back of my head and fists my hair, I feel his need.

This isn't a goodbye kiss.

It can't be.

I raise my arms and gasp for air as Wes pulls my hoodie and tank top off over my head in one motion. Then, I dive for his mouth again. The only time I feel truly alive is when I'm kissing this man. He's like a live wire—calm and quiet on the outside but a raging electrical storm within. One touch, and I'm rooted to the spot, lit up and blazing hot as his power surges through me. It scrambles my thoughts, blasts through all my fears, and leaves me humming and vibrating and yearning for more.

Wes strips himself of his shirt, holster, and tank top. Then, as soon as his hands are free, they reach for me. Rough palms caress my exposed skin and tear at the clothes preventing them from touching more. Wes yanks my lacy bra down around my waist and feasts on the curve of my neck as he kneads my aching breasts. I arch my back and cling to the ladder rung above my head as his soft, warm mouth trails wet kisses down my chest. All I can do is hold on, paralyzed by the current of pleasure flowing through me, as Wes swirls and sucks and drags his tongue over each of my tight, tender nipples.

He places one of my feet on his thigh and makes quick work of my bootlaces. In a few seconds, both of my hiking boots join the growing pile of clothes on the ground, and Wes's hands move straight to my zipper. I go to reach for him, but he places my hand back on the wooden slat above me.

"Don't move," he growls, yanking my jeans and panties down my thighs. "I want you just like this."

Once I'm completely naked, Wes takes a step back and admires me. Stretched out on the ladder. Arms up. Back arched. Breasts wet from his mouth and heaving with my every breath.

Even in the dark of the bookstore and behind that curtain of brown hair, I see the moment his eyes darken. A shiver cascades down my spine as Wes licks his full bottom lip and unfastens his jeans. I swallow as his thumbs hook into his waistband, shoving his pants and boxers down just enough to free himself, and I feel my heart sink as his hand wraps around his hard cock.

I wanted to make love to Wes.

But it looks like the Ice King just took his place.

Wes's eyes don't meet mine as he stalks toward me. They linger on my body as he strokes his length. Even though my heart is breaking, slick heat trickles between my thighs as my back arches toward his ghost. I'll take this man any way I can get him even if the version I'm getting isn't him at all.

"Fuck," Wes hisses, snaking his hands down my sides, over my hips, and around to squeeze my full ass.

Wes spreads me apart as he pulls my body toward him, guiding his thickness into the slippery mess between my thighs. He groans, pushing my hips away from him and pulling them right back. I hold on to the ladder with both hands as he drags his smooth flesh between my folds. His head is bowed as he watches himself disappear between my thighs.

He won't look at me.

He won't even look at me.

"Wes," I cry, my voice breaking with need.

His eyes snap up, softened by surprise, and I catch a glimmer of the man inside. Reaching out with one hand, I cup his hard jaw, holding it in place so that he can't look away.

"Stay with me," I beg, my eyes darting back and forth between his. I hope he hears me. I hope he feels all the ways that I mean those words.

Hooking my thigh over his hip, Wes presses the tip of himself against the core of me. He blinks, but he doesn't look away as he fills me slowly. His pale green eyes are a tortured mix of agony and ecstasy as they bore into mine, but they're honest, and they're open, and for once, they do as I say.

They stay.

Wes's jaw muscles flex beneath my fingertips as we click into place, and for a moment, we're as close as two people can be. The intensity of that stare is paralyzing. The feeling of his bare skin against mine, intoxicating. The heat of his breath and the thump of his heart and the pulsing need where we're joined are overwhelming.

Then, he closes his eyes.

He withdraws.

And when he thrusts forward again, it's not sweet and slow.

It's hard and cold.

Wes's fingertips bite into my thigh, holding me in place as his hips surge forward in deep, punctuated, violent motions. He's fucking me like he's stabbing me. Like he's trying to rid himself of his pain by burying it in my flesh.

So, I cling to the wooden rung above my head and take it. All of it.

Because Wes's pain still feels better than mine.

His eyebrows crease, and his lips part. And all I want to do is make whatever he's feeling go away. So, I lean forward and do the only thing there is left to do. I press a kiss to his perfect lips.

Wes stills for a moment. Then, he wraps his arms around my body so tight that I can hardly breathe. He devours my mouth, taking everything I have to give as he fills me to my limit.

Wrapping my arms around his neck, I coil my right leg around his waist for support as he grinds against my over-sensitized flesh. I was wrong before. *This* is as close as two people can get.

Wes isn't showing me his brave face or his guarded face. He isn't showing me his face at all.

He's showing me his fear.

The moment I feel him swell and jerk inside of me, my body detonates, contracting around him suddenly and violently. I whimper into his mouth with every surge of pleasure and swallow his quiet moans of pain.

He doesn't pull out, doesn't break our connection. He holds me and kisses me until he's making love to me again, and I'm hit with a sickening sense of déjà vu.

This is exactly how he made love to me yesterday up in my tree house—passionately, endlessly—as if it were our last night on earth.

I didn't think this was a goodbye kiss, but maybe I was wrong.

Because the last time Wes tried to tell me goodbye, it felt exactly like this.

Wes

It's DARK AS NIGHT up in the tree house, but I don't need light to see Rain. She fucking glows. The blunt edge of her black hair, the straight line of her nose, the curves of her body, and the overlap of her arms across her chest. I can see every swoop and bend of her in perfect detail.

I'm fucking obsessed.

Which is why I need to go right the fuck now.

I drape Rain's clothes over her naked, napping body, tuck her hoodie under her head, and place my pocketknife in her tiny fist. She grips it and pulls it close as I kiss her on the forehead one last time. I let my lips linger, inhaling the fading scent of vanilla on her skin just to torture myself. Then, I climb out of the tree house with a noose of emotion wrapped around my neck.

Leave before you get left has never fucking hurt like this.

I have to get out of here before I do something stupid, like change my mind. I won't be able to breathe again until this place is a blip in my rearview—along with the girl who almost got me. Fool me once, shame on you. Do that shit thirteen more times, and guess what. I'm motherfucking foolproof.

I throw my clothes back on, check to make sure I still have the key to the Ninja in my pocket, and look around for the backpack.

Goddamn it.

I stomp out of the bookstore and try to focus on how disgusting this place is instead of the growing black hole in my chest. The floor is covered in trash and dust and cracked tiles with weeds growing in between them. The walls are covered with graffiti and shittily drawn dicks. And I can hear fucking frogs croaking somewhere in the atrium.

Frogs.

I turn left at the petri dish of a fountain and head straight to the tuxedo shop.

Rain's backpack is sitting on the counter, right where she left it, so I unzip it and dig around for what I need. I'm only going to take my antibiotics, a few bandages, maybe a protein bar or two, and a bottle of water. I can find the rest when I get back to town. I pocket the pills and shove a beige brick of food into my mouth, not even bothering to taste it as I hunt for the water bottles. When I find them, they're both empty.

Whatever. I'll just find a house with a garden hose on my—

The sound of moaning and coughing behind the counter scatters my thoughts.

Don't look. He's not your problem. This is the same guy who pulled a rifle on you in the hardware store, remember? Fuck him.

I look anyway.

Fuck me.

Quint's dark eyes are wide open, and his chest is heaving like he just ran a marathon. He tries to sit up, winces, and falls back to the ground as his hand flies up to touch his neck.

"No!" I leap over the counter and grab his wrist before he does any damage.

His brother is sitting next to him, passed out cold with his head against the checkout stand cabinets.

Quint's wild eyes lock on to mine.

"You're okay, man," I say, placing his hand on his chest, but from this close, I can see that he is definitely not fucking okay.

His skin is hot to the touch and covered in beads of sweat. His lips are chapped and pale. His shirt is soaked. And a trickle of blood is seeping from the bandage with every panicked pulse of his jugular.

Quint opens his mouth to try to ask me something but winces again as the glass shifts from the motion.

I glance at Lamar and debate whether or not to wake him up, but the kid has been on twenty-four-hour watch since we got here and could use the fucking shut-eye.

"Don't try to talk, okay? You were in an accident. We couldn't get you back to Franklin Springs, so we brought you to Pritchard Park Mall. You're in the old Savvi Formalwear right now. That's pretty boss, right?"

Quint tries to smile but cringes and bites his bottom lip from the pain.

Shit.

"You took some glass to the neck, man, but Rain's got you patched up. She'll be by to check on you in a few, okay?"

Quint grabs my wrist and looks at me with eyes the color of my cold, dead heart.

"Am I …" he whispers, pausing to suck in a breath and grimace from the pain.

"Hell no," I lie. "Don't even say it. You're gonna be fine."

Quint squeezes his eyes shut and grits his teeth as his face crumples. A high-pitched keening sound comes from

63

somewhere deep inside his body, and I can't fucking take it anymore.

"You're gonna be okay," I say more forcefully, but I don't know who I'm trying to convince—myself or Quint. "You want some water? I'm gonna get you some water."

I stand up and grab the empty bottles on my way out the door.

Fuck.

This.

Place.

I have to concentrate on not crushing the plastic bottles in my fists as I stomp toward the food court.

Fuck.

These.

People.

A fat-ass toad jumps from the edge of the fountain into the murky, mucous-like water inside as I pass.

Supplies.

Shelter.

Self-defense.

I kick a broken tile.

I'm getting this motherfucker some water.

Then, I'm getting the fuck out of here.

The second I walk into the food court, I set my sights on the bitch at the back table. Q. She and the rest of her minions are still celebrating the end of civilization. A few tattooed misfits with random parts of their heads shaved are playing cards and taking shots from a bottle of bottom-shelf tequila. A beanpole in a jean jacket with the sleeves cut off is playing a goddamn accordion while a burly, bearded guy in a pair of unwashed overalls strums along on the banjo. A few crusty teens are gathered around a cell phone, elbowing each other like they're watching porn, and Q is kicked back in a plastic chair, smoking a joint, with a busted pair of black motorcycle boots propped up on the table and her black men's pants cut off at the knees.

Fucking gutter punks.

"Well, well, well." Q coughs, holding the smoke in her lungs. "If it ain't our new roomie, *Hawaii Five-0*. Everybody say, 'Hi, *Hawaii Five-0*.'"

"Hi, *Hawaii Five-0*," the clan drawls without looking up.

"Where's the luau?" Q exhales and passes the joint to her right.

I want to bark at her that I don't have time for her bullshit, but I smirk through my rage and hold up the empty water bottles. "Know where I can fill these?"

Q gets an evil glimmer in her gangrene-colored eyes and sits forward. She drops her feet to the floor and sits with her legs spread wide apart, like a dude.

"Water's for employees only, Surfer Boy." Q eyes me up and down. Her eyebrows and eyelashes are thick and dark. Her brownish-greenish-yellowish dreadlocks are flipped over the top of her head, spilling over one shoulder and ending somewhere below the full tits she's hiding underneath that baggy T-shirt. And the gold hoop in her nose glints in the light as she grins, deciding she likes what she sees.

I don't need this shit.

"You know what? I'll find it somewhere else. Thanks."

I turn to leave, but the sound of Q's plastic chair scraping the ground stops me in my tracks.

"Hold up."

I look at her over my shoulder with my *not interested in your bullshit* face firmly in place.

"Let's take a little field trip. I wanna show you somethin'."

"I don't have time for—"

"Listen, muhfucka. I let you stay in my castle last night. I gave you my protection from the Bonys. I fuckin' fed yo' ass. You can give me five minutes."

She's right. I might not like this bitch, but right now, she's the best resource I've got.

"Fine. Five."

"I'm sorry. I think what you meant to say is, *Thank you, Yo Majesty*." Q stands and brushes her dreads over her shoulder with a dramatic sweep of her hand.

"Thanks," I mutter as Q turns and walks away from the table, gesturing for me to follow her with a flick of her long-ass fingernails.

"We gon' have to work on that last part." She cackles over her shoulder.

I feel the eyes of everyone in the food court on my back as we walk across the room and through a swinging half-door next to one of the fast-food counters.

"You ever see *Charlie and the Chocolate Factory*, Surfer Boy?"

"Uh, yeah. Why?" I mutter as we turn down a series of skinny, unlit hallways behind the restaurant kitchens.

Q pulls the latch on a heavy metal door and yanks it open, revealing a set of metal stairs. "Because I'm about to show you the April 23 version." Q grins and gestures for me to go up the stairs first.

Fuck it. Here we go, down the rabbit hole.

I can't see shit in the stairwell, but after what I found at the top of the last dark staircase I climbed, I'm pretty sure whatever I'm about to see couldn't possibly be worse. When I get to the landing at the top, I reach my hands out in front of me and feel the smooth surface of a metal door.

"Open it," Q says behind me, so I find the handle and give it a shove.

When the door swings open, the sun slaps me in the face so hard that it damn near blinds me. I lift my forearm to shield my eyes, and Q chuckles behind me.

"Go on."

I step out onto the roof, and the first thing I notice is the sound of birds clucking ... just before something huge goes flapping past my face.

"The fuck?" I drop my hand and squint in the direction that it traveled, finding a flying fucking hen landing on the roof of a plastic playhouse surrounded by chicken wire.

At least six more fat-ass chickens are inside the makeshift coop, staring at me with shifty orange eyes.

"That one's Asshole." Q nods toward the ball of feathers that almost took my head off. "We let her out during the day because ... well, she's a fuckin' asshole if we don't."

I look around in disbelief. Q was right. This place is insane. They have rows and rows of blue plastic rain barrels, dozens of containers—everything from old washing machines to tires—spilling over with fruits and vegetables, some of the biggest pot plants I've ever seen, and beyond the junk yard of a garden is a giant inflatable pool surrounded by mismatched patio furniture.

"You did all this?" I ask, trying to ignore the chicken staring at me in my peripheral vision.

"Hell nah." Q snorts, wrinkling up her nose. "I told you, I'm the queen up in here. I don't do shit. My people did all this." Q sweeps her hand out over her dominion as she turns and walks down the path separating the water collection area from the garden.

"Where did you guys get all this stuff?" I ask, following a few feet behind her.

Q shrugs. "Walmart."

I snort out a laugh as she comes to a stop next to a propane camping stove by the water barrels.

"Lysol used to sneak over there with a pair of bolt cutters every few days to steal shit outta the lawn and garden section. Opie used to swipe chickens and tools and shit from a farm somewhere around here. And Pizza Face yanked that pool right outta some kid's backyard."

"Those your *scouts*?"

"Were. Until the Bonys showed up." Something flashes across Q's face before she flicks her fingers at the teakettle sitting on top of the single-burner stove. "You gotta boil that shit before you drink it ..."

"I thought you said water was for employees."

"That's why I brought you up here, Surfer Boy." Q points off into the distance. "You see that pharmacy, 'bout two blocks down? Now, Bonys already done broke into it, but I know there's gotta be some good shit left. You scope it out for me; I'll give you all the water you can drink. Bring me back some tampons and toilet paper …" Q's catlike eyes drift south as the corner of one angled eyebrow crawls north. "I'll be ya best muhfuckin' friend."

I open my mouth to tell her I'm not staying, but something she said makes me bite my tongue.

There's a pharmacy.

Right across the fucking street.

I sigh and scrub a hand down my face. "Fine. But I'm gonna need that water up front."

Wes

TWO BLOCKS.

I sling Rain's empty backpack over my good shoulder and push open the exit door. I might be an asshole, but even I can't let a guy die on the floor of an abandoned mall without at least checking the pharmacy down the street for meds first.

God, you better be watching. I deserve some serious extra credit for this shit.

The sun is already beginning to slide behind the pines next to the exit ramp, so I pick up the pace as I walk across the parking lot. I listen for the sound of motorcycles, gunshots, dogs barking, *anything*, but it's eerily quiet. The road in front of the mall has a few vehicles on it, but they're still and silent.

Instead of engines and car horns, all I hear are birds and broken glass under my feet.

It looks like an urban wasteland out here. It sounds like a goddamn nature preserve. And, for a moment, it feels like I really am the last asshole on earth.

This is exactly how I pictured April 24. No people. No rent. No debate about whether to stay or leave anybody or anyplace. Just me and the shit of the earth.

Only in my head, it felt a hell of a lot better than this.

I step over a section of flattened chain-link fence and look down the street in both directions. The pharmacy is so close that I could be there in about two minutes if I stuck to the road, but considering that the last bastard I saw walk down this highway is still lying on it about fifty yards away, I decide to cross the street and walk behind a strip shopping center instead.

I draw my gun as I slide along the side of the brick building, taking care not to let the gravel crunch too loudly under my boots. The farther away I get from the street, the worse the smell. I dismiss it as just another overflowing dumpster—until I recognize it.

It's the same way Rain's house smelled when I found her parents.

My stomach twists and my heart pounds as I take a breath and glance around the corner of the building.

Yep.

There's a dead body back there all right.

A dead body being chewed on by a pack of fucking dogs.

I stifle a gag, but the noise in the back of my throat doesn't go unnoticed. One head pops up from the pack. Then, another. And another. By the time the first bark sounds, I'm in a full sprint and already halfway to the dumpster behind the building. I grab the top edge and swing myself up as a dozen mangy dogs descend upon me. Thank fuck the lid was closed. The dogs bark and snarl and rake their claws down the sides of the metal box I'm standing on while I catch my breath and try not to look at the carcass on the ground a few feet away.

Think, motherfucker.

I glance to the right. The pharmacy is next to the shopping center, separated by a parking lot, but it's too damn far to make a run for it. I have no food—I emptied the backpack before I left so that I could fit more supplies inside of it—and I am *not* shooting a bunch of golden retrievers and Labradoodles.

One of the dogs yelps and bucks a smaller dog off its back. *Fuck, they're trying to climb each other now.*

Climb …

I hold my breath as I look down the length of the building. Then, I exhale when I spot what I'm looking for.

A fire escape.

The ladder is about forty feet away though.

More yelps and growls break out below as I try to figure out how to distract these guys long enough to make it across the pavement. Half of them still have their collars on, so I know they haven't been wild for long. I bet if I had a tennis ball, most of them would still chase it.

They're not predators; they're just fucking starving.

A breeze blows through the alley behind the shopping center, causing the stench of death and whatever's decomposing in the dumpster to intensify. I pull my shirt over my nose and mouth, trying like hell to keep from puking, when my eyes land on a sign next to one of the metal back doors.

Parkside Bakery.

Bakery.

Food!

Before I even finish formulating my plan, I drop to my knees, reach down into the dog soup below me, grab the handle on the sliding side door of the dumpster, and yank that motherfucker open.

The bastards go insane, clawing and jumping and climbing over one another to try to get inside. I pull my hand back just as a Jack Russell terrier with gnashing teeth makes it to the top of the dogpile. He chomps down on a paper bag just inside the open door and rips it open with a violent shake of his head. I don't wait to see what comes falling out. Whatever it is, it's enough to keep them distracted as I leap to the ground and take off for the ladder.

I grit my teeth and try not to look at the battered body on the ground as I sprint past it, but the sight of purple dreadlocks in my peripheral vision tells me more than I wanted to know.

I'm not the first scout Q has sent on this mission.

Bile climbs up my throat, but I push it down and run harder. When I make it to the ladder without being chased, I decide to keep running. I don't stop to look both ways before I cross the parking lot between the shopping center and the pharmacy, and I don't fucking slow down. I'm done being cautious. I'm done with this whole goddamn day. I just want to get in, get out, and get the fuck out of Pritchard Park forever.

I draw my gun and duck through the shattered sliding glass door. Usually, I would tiptoe around in case someone was inside, but honestly, I *hope* someone's inside. There's a rage building inside of me that I wouldn't mind unleashing on a Day-Glo skeleton right about now.

Fuck Quint for getting hurt.

Fuck Carter for having a pulse.

Fuck the World Health Assholes for doing this to us.

Fuck Q for sending me on this goddamn death march.

Fuck Rain for making me want to believe in shit that history has proven will never fucking exist for me.

"If anybody's in here, come the fuck out!" I snarl, sweeping my head from left to right. The place is silent. "You have three seconds to show yourself, or I will shoot your ass on sight!"

When I don't hear anything, except for the blood rushing in my ears from the run and my untapped wrath, I do a quick survey of what's left in the store. The checkout station has been ransacked. There's not a single pack of cigarettes, candy bar, or bag of chips left on the shelves, but the rest of the store looks pretty much the same.

I guess makeup and greeting cards aren't exactly a top priority when you think the world's about to end.

The pharmacy is in the back corner, past all the convenience store bullshit, so I unzip the backpack and make my way down the aisles, chucking shit in along the way. Tampons, toothpaste, shampoo, hand sanitizer, protein bars, peanut butter ... I can't believe all this stuff is still here. In Franklin Springs, this place would have been taken over by thugs weeks ago.

Oh shit.

The realization stops me in my tracks and then sends me sprinting past everything else in the store and diving over the pharmacy counter.

The Bonys probably *did* have guys posted in here twenty-four/seven ... up until yesterday. They thought the world was gonna end just like everybody else, so they were out, getting fucked up and killing pedestrians for fun. I saw them. But when they finally shake off their hangovers and figure out that the world didn't end and it was all just a hoax ...

The rumble of motorcycle engines in the distance fuels me as I scour the labels on row after row of identical white bottles with incomprehensible Latin words printed on them.

Goddamn it!

I don't know what any of this means. Nobody ever took me to the doctor as a kid. The only drugs I know are the ones with street value, and of course, those are long gone.

Rain would know what to look for.

Rain.

I unzip the front pouch on her backpack and read the label on the pills she swiped from Carter's house for my bullet wound.

KEFLEX (cephalexin) Capsules, 250 mg

I kiss the label and drop the almost-empty bottle back into the bag. The roaring of engines grows louder as I scan the shelves for anything starting with a K.

Forget about the drugs! Run, dumbass!

Epinephrine ... flurazepam ...

Go! Now!

Glucophage ... hydralazine ...

What are you doing? Do you think that Quint kid would be up in here, finding meds for you right now? Fucking run!

Keppra—no. Shit. Too far … Keflex!

The moment my fingers graze the five-hundred-count bottle of antibiotics, the crunch of broken glass under boot heels roots me to the spot.

"Argh!" a deep voice growls just before the sound of something being smashed echoes off the high ceiling. "They took all the goddamn smokes!"

I crouch down on the floor between two pharmacy shelves as a second pair of feet comes crunching into the store.

"Ah, man," a younger voice says, so quietly I can barely hear him. "They took all the Mr. Goodbars."

"Fuck Mr. Goodbar!" the older asshole yells, followed by the sound of hollow cardboard containers tumbling to the ground. "If you don't find me a cigarette, a cuppa coffee, and something for this gotdamn migraine in the next five minutes, I'ma beat yer ass, boy."

"I—"

"Four minutes!"

"Okay, fine."

I unzip the backpack, tooth by plastic tooth, and slide the Keflex bottle in as quietly as possible.

"I'ma check the break room for a coffeepot," the older asshole grumbles. "Anybody tries to come in that door … shoot 'em."

Shit.

I look around, frantically trying to find a better place to hide. The shelves of drugs run perpendicular to the pharmacy counter, so even though I'm crouched down, anyone walking by would be able to see me. The only safe place would be under the counter, but with all the shit in this backpack, there's no way I could get over there without making noise.

So, I do the only thing I can; I wrap both hands around the smooth wooden handle of Rain's dad's .44 Magnum, and I say a silent prayer to my new pal, God.

"Hey, Vipe, I found a carton of Virginia Slims!"

"I ain't smokin' no *Vagina Slimes!*" The asshole's voice is much louder than before.

Closer.

Every muscle in my body tenses, including my trigger finger, as the old bastard walks into view. His thinning gray hair is pulled back in a low ponytail. His leathery skin is pockmarked and sunburned. His beer gut sticks a solid foot out in front of him, and his black biker jacket has been spray-painted with neon-orange stripes resembling skeleton bones.

He stops right in front of the counter, and my finger tightens around the trigger. But he doesn't see me. Instead, he turns his back and pulls a bottle of Excedrin off the shelf across from the pharmacy counter.

"Maybe I should grab some Vagisil for that pussy of yours while I'm back here." He cough-laughs into his fist while I stare down the barrel of my gun, aiming directly for his bald spot.

My heart is pounding so hard I can feel every vein pulse and swell as they force the blood into my muscles. I know this feeling. This is exactly how I used to feel every single night, lying in an unfamiliar bed, clutching whatever weapon I'd stashed under my pillow, waiting for some other balding, beer-gutted piece of shit to come find me.

The bloated Bony pops the cap on the Excedrin bottle and tosses a few into his mouth before turning his head toward something out of my view.

"What you doin', boy?"

"I'm just gonna grab some allergy meds. This pollen is killin' me."

"The *pollen* is killin' you?"

The hungover old fuck shakes his head, and I know what's coming next before it even happens. He's gonna call that kid a little bitch and throw that bottle of Excedrin at him.

He turns his head sideways, so I aim for his temple.

"The pollen's killin' you?" He raises his voice, cocks his arm back, and lets the painkillers fly. I hear them bounce off of something before hitting the ground with a rattle. "How the fuck did I end up with a pussy wipe for a son? I shoulda put a pillow over your face the day your mama shit you out!"

My fingers tighten around the gun in my hands; I wish it were that motherfucker's neck.

"Sorry, sir," the kid mumbles.

"Get the fuck outta my sight!" the dickhead yells, throwing his hand in the direction of the pharmacy.

Shit.

Even though there are about three aisles of drugs between the pharmacy door and me, they're open shelving units. I can see everything. I see the door handle slowly rotate down. I see the door swing open with a creak. I see the ripped jeans, black-and-orange skeleton hoodie, and shaggy hair of a kid who can't be older than fourteen.

His posture is hunched over, as if he wants to curl in on himself until he disappears, and he's too busy staring at the floor to notice the man hiding in plain sight ten feet away.

Something on the shelf in front of him catches his attention, and he leans over even further to pick a small purple box off the shelf.

Zyrtec. Thank fuck.

Take it and go. Take it ... and ...

The kid's eyes lift suddenly, as if I'd spoken out loud, and lock directly on to mine.

Well, one of them does.

The other one is swollen shut and black as hell.

His good eye goes wide as it lands on my gun, so I quickly lower it and raise a finger to my lips.

Please don't make me shoot you, kid. For fuck's sake ...

The boy bristles but not because of me. Because of the sound of footsteps in the hallway behind him.

"Hey, you little cocksucker ..." Daddy Dearest appears in the doorway, and I can smell last night's liquor on him from here. "You find a coffeepot back h—"

His beady, bloodshot eyes drift from his cowering son to whatever—or whoever—the kid is staring at, and the second they land on me, I'm on my feet. Backpack in one hand, gun in the other, I sprint for the counter, hoping to clear it before the bastard can get a clean shot on me, but the sound of skin hitting skin stops me in my tracks.

The man shouts a few choice expletives at the kid, but I can't hear them. All I can hear is that backhand. It reverberates through my jaw, just like it did the first time *I* got hit in the mouth. The sting of pain, followed by the burn of humiliation.

Words like, "Shoot him, stupid," and, "Give me that fuckin' gun. *I'll* do it," slide off my back and land on the floor in a meaningless pile of syllables as I turn and face every motherfucker who ever put his hands on me, all rolled into one.

The rage that has been building inside of me all day now feels like a tiny match … that just got dropped into a can of gasoline.

I surrender all control of my body—give it over willingly—and watch like a spectator as I charge straight toward that piece of shit. His rodent-like eyes widen in shock just before my shoulder careens into his bloated fucking belly, sending him stumbling backward into the wall.

The noises make it to my brain first—something plastic clattering to the ground, boots shuffling over dirty floors, the dull smack of knuckles hitting teeth, the melodic ping of those teeth hitting the tiles—and then the physical sensations begin to come through. The rush of adrenaline through my bloodstream, the crunching pain in my right hand every time it connects with his face, the delicious strain of muscles in my left arm as I fight to keep him upright against the wall. Vaguely, I register his flailing arms, his dirty fingers trying to punch and poke whatever parts of me he can reach, but he can't hurt me.

Nobody can.

Not anymore.

A new sound rises over the pounding of blood in my ears, and it pulls me back to reality like a bucket of cold water.

It's a small, cracking voice demanding in an unconvincing tone that I, "Stand back."

Fuck. The kid.

I release his old man and step back with my hands in the air as the bastard's limp body slides down the wall.

"Back up," he says again, pointing a .32 at me with shaking hands.

I do as he said, my knuckles screaming in pain and my chest expanding violently with every breath I suck in.

"'Bout fuckin' time, you piece of shit," the old man spits through the fleshy pulp that used to be his lips. His eyes are swollen to mush. A river of blood runs from his broken nose down his mouth and chin. And when he rolls his head toward the kid, he garbles, "Shoot him, stupi—" but he doesn't get a chance to finish his command.

A bullet above his right eye shuts him up forever.

I flinch as the blast echoes around me. I turn with my hands still raised and face the corpse's maker. His posture is taller, his good eye narrowed in resolve.

He's not looking at me when he lowers his gun, and he's not speaking to me when he says—no, declares—"I'm. Not. Stupid."

The heat of the moment changes from charged and frenetic to stifling and heavy.

This is the world we live in now.

No social workers were coming to help this kid.

No Department of Child and Family Services.

No cops or judges or family attorneys were gonna fight for him.

And there won't be any coming to investigate this crime scene either.

This is the new justice system.

And right now, I'm scared to ask myself which one is better.

The kid finally looks at me, shock giving way to shame as he awaits my judgment, but I have none to give him.

Instead, I grab my backpack—pain shooting through almost every muscle, knuckle, and rib in my body—and head toward him on my way out the door.

I pause right before I pass, placing a hesitant hand on the kid's trembling shoulder. "Fuck 'em," I spit out, my eyes fixed on the empty hallway beyond the door and the empty life waiting for me beyond that. "Say *fuck 'em* and survive anyway."

April 25
Rain

I WAKE FROM A dreamless sleep, only to find myself lying in a pitch-black nightmare.

When I sit up and blink into the darkness of the tree house, my shirt tumbles off my bare chest and lands in my lap. My right hip is sore as hell from lying on the plywood floor. I rub it absentmindedly as I wait for my eyes to adjust to the darkness. I must have slept all the way through the afternoon and into the night. There isn't a speck of daylight filtering in from the hallway anymore.

But I don't need light to know that Wes is gone.

I can feel it.

His heat, his scent, his quiet, simmering intensity—all of it. Gone. The only evidence that he was even here are the clothes draped over my naked body and the pocketknife tucked into my fist.

He might as well have stabbed it into my heart.

I squeeze the textured handle as hard as I can. I squeeze it until my fingernails cut into my palm and my biceps begin to shake. I squeeze it even harder than I squeeze my eyes shut as I fight to keep the tears at bay.

Supplies. Shelter. Self-defense.

Wes left me with the last thing he thought I needed to survive.

Without him.

Stop it. Maybe he just had to pee. Maybe he went to find water.

I pull my shirt on over my head and feel around for my jeans.

Oh God. Maybe he's in trouble.

Worry swallows my despair and sends me scrambling down the tree house ladder. I trip over my boots at the bottom, pausing just long enough to shove my feet into them.

My vision adjusts to the dark, allowing me to avoid the edges and corners of the bookshelves as I trudge past. My footsteps sound flat and heavy, as if the grief I'm carrying has actual weight.

Please let him be okay. Please, God. I'll do anything.

The hallway is silent, except for the occasional cricket or frog, but I shatter that silence with every puddle I accidentally splash through and every broken tile I send skidding across the filthy floor.

My brain lies to me, my eyes seeing Hawaiian prints and haunting eyes in every reflection and shadow I pass. When they finally land on the fountain, I gasp as the silhouette of a man rises beside it. Hope fills my heart and then gushes out through a fresh tear when the figure lifts a rifle to his shoulder.

"Don't shoot." I hold my hands up. "It's Rain."

"Holy shit, Rain! You're still here?" Carter's voice echoes through the atrium as he lowers his weapon and jogs toward me.

When his long arms pull me to his chest, another wave of déjà vu from last night crashes over me. Carter hugged me like this before he knew that Wes and I were together. When he still thought I was his.

The only reason he would hug me like that now is if—

"He's gone, isn't he?"

Carter's body goes stiff. Then, he nods against the top of my head.

"Nobody's seen him since yesterday afternoon. Or you." Carter drops his arms and takes a step back so that he can look down at me. "But here you are."

I can't see his face, but I know he's smiling from the tone of his voice.

Wes is missing, and Carter's smiling.

I take a step back, too. "Does anyone know where he went? We have to find him, Carter. What if he's hurt?"

"He's not fucking hurt," Carter huffs, turning to walk toward the fountain. He leans over and lifts something off the ground. It's about the size and shape of a small boulder.

"I found this tonight while I was patrolling." He points a finger at the south hall. "Just inside the main entrance."

Carter hands me the large bundle. It's heavy in my arms and rough against my skin, but it's not the feel that tells me I'm holding my own backpack; it's the smell. The subtle scent of Daddy's cigarettes and Mama's hazelnut coffee that used to linger on everything it touched in the house. It hits me like a sucker punch, stealing my breath and making my eyes burn.

"It's full of supplies." Carter's tone is smug and accusing. "I knew it was yours because of the keychain hanging from the zipper. At first, I thought you must have dropped it off for Quint before you left, but since you're still here—"

"He left it for me."

Carter has the decency to shut his mouth as I hug the overstuffed bag to my chest.

It's fitting that it's so full. It's as if everything I've lost is crammed inside.

My parents. My home. My old life.

My Wes.

I smell them on the canvas, feel the weight of them in my arms.

But they're not here.

They're gone, and they're never coming back.

I make it to the edge of the fountain before my knees buckle. Curling my body around the backpack, I slide to the floor, holding on to it for dear life as I rock back and forth.

My eyes are fixed on nothing, and that's exactly what I feel.

Nothingness.

It is deep and wide and dark and damp.

It smells like stale cigarettes and morning coffee.

It swirls, like cemetery fog, around me. Clouding my vision. Numbing my pain.

None of this matters, it whispers. It always knows just what to say.

But then I feel something else wrap around me. Something warm and solid and wonderful.

He is heavy, like the backpack, but grounding.

He smells like home too, in his own way.

He is real, and he is here, and when I look up at the tender concern in his eyes, the fog lifts.

And the pain comes. It rips through me like a rusty machete as I bury my face in Carter's T-shirt, as my emotions decide they've found a safe place to go and flee my body in torrents.

I cry and mourn and twist my fists in the soft cotton while Carter shushes me and pulls me closer.

Which only makes me cry harder.

Not because of everything I've lost.

But because of the one thing I actually got back.

My best friend.

"Carter?" a shaky voice calls from the end of the hall leading toward the main entrance.

"Yeah?" he replies into the darkness, clearing his throat.

"I don't know what to do, man. He's ... he's gettin' worse."

"Lamar?" I wipe my eyes and sit up.

"Rainbow?" The elation in Lamar's voice surprises me. "Rainbow! You're still here!"

The sound of sneakers pounding the tiles echoes down the hall, reaching me seconds before he does.

"You gotta come. Right now. He's ... I can't ... I don't ... you gotta help him, Rainbow. Please!" Lamar's voice cracks, reminding me just how young he is.

Fourteen? Fifteen maybe?

I've been so caught up in my own shit that I never stopped to think how hard all this must be for him. Underneath all that attitude, he's still just a kid.

I hold out my hands and let him pull me to my feet, missing the warmth of Carter's arm around my shoulders the moment it falls away. I know without turning around that he'll bring my backpack.

He always used to carry it for me at school.

As Lamar tugs me toward the tuxedo shop, I notice the first traces of morning light peeking in through the broken windows in the main entrance doors. They illuminate the doorway of the Hello Kitty store where Wes told me he'd never fight to keep me from leaving.

If only I had fought harder to make him stay.

Or maybe I should have agreed to leave with him, like he wanted me to, I think as I follow Lamar into the tuxedo shop, but when I come around the end of the counter and see Quint's body convulsing on the floor, I know that's not true.

This is exactly where I'm supposed to be.

In fact, this is the only place I *want* to be.

No smells. No triggers. No angry mobs. No dead bodies.

In here, I have a purpose. In here, I have friends. Out there ...

In my mind, I reopen the fortress of Shit I'm Not Going to Think About Ever Again Because None of This Matters and We're All Going to Die, take everything outside those doors— my old house, the bodies buried in fresh dirt behind it, the beautiful boy in the Hawaiian shirt who saved my life and broke my heart, motorcycles and loose dogs and tree houses and burning buildings—and shove it all inside.

Then, I unzip the backpack Carter set on the counter, and I get to work.

May 1 (One Week Later)
Rain

"YOU ATE YOUR BREAKFAST!" Carter's cheerful voice shatters the silence in the tuxedo shop as his six-foot-three frame fills the doorway.

"Yeah …" Quint clears his throat. "Kep' it down this time, too."

Carter's bright face darkens as his eyes flick from mine to the boy sitting next to me behind the counter.

"That's great, man," he replies with a smile that only I know is fake.

I know all his smiles.

"Has your *nurse* eaten anything today?" Carter's gaze slides over to me.

Quint shrugs as I drop my eyes and pull the sleeves of my hooded sweatshirt over my hands.

Carter presses his full lips into a thin line and nods slightly.

Thanks to the antibiotics, hand sanitizer, and gauze I found in my backpack, I was able to kill Quint's infection, remove the glass from his neck, and by some miracle, keep him from bleeding out while I bandaged him up, but knowing that Wes was the one who had delivered those supplies only made the festering stab wound in my own heart grow deeper.

"Rain ... can I talk to you outside?"

I lock my hoodie sleeves in my fists and shake my head.

"Not *outside*, outside, just ... in the hallway."

Quint gives me a nudge with his elbow. "Go on, girl. You ain't left this room in days. I'll be a'ight."

With a huff, I pull myself to stand. Every muscle in my body rejoices over finally being used as I follow Carter out the door. Once I'm in the hallway, I lean against the wall outside the tuxedo shop and stare straight ahead.

"You're not even gonna look at me?"

"I will ... if you stand over here." I gesture toward the wall across from me with a hoodie-covered fist and then press my knuckles to my lips. The black cotton doesn't smell like home anymore.

Thank God.

"Uh ... okay?" Carter pads into view with his hands in his pockets and his eyebrows raised in uncertainty. "This better?"

I nod.

"I guess that answers my question."

"What question?" I mumble into my hoodie sleeve.

"I have an errand to run. I thought it might be fun if you came with, but seeing as how you won't even *look* at the exit, I'm guessing that's a no."

"Yeah, that's a no. Are we done?" I close my eyes as I turn to go back into the tuxedo shop, not wanting to accidentally catch a glimpse of what's outside those doors. In my mind, it's all gone. And that's exactly how I want it to stay.

"Rain ..."

Carter's long fingers wrap around my bicep, and I go limp, letting him pull me against his chest without an ounce of protest. I hate how badly I need his hugs. Anyone's hugs.

"You haven't eaten anything in days. You haven't left the mall since you got here. Hell, you've barely even left the tuxedo shop. All you do is obsess over Quint and Lamar. I get that you want to help and all, but you need to take a break and get some fresh air before you lose your shit."

"This air is good enough."

"Maybe we could take a walk around here and then … go say hi to my folks? They've been asking about you."

"Well, you can tell 'em I'm right here." I straighten my spine and take a step backward out of his embrace.

Carter runs a hand through his loose curls in exasperation. Then, his eyes widen and lips curve with the makings of what is probably a bad idea. "You know what? I'm gonna do that. Be right back."

I watch him walk away with long, determined strides before I shuffle back to the safety of Savvi Formalwear.

Inside, Quint gives me a smirk. I wrapped his neck in so much gauze that it looks like he's wearing a diaper as a necklace. His eyes are sunken, and his lips are dry. But the fact that he's vertical and smiling feels like a handful of glitter sprinkled on top of the stagnant black cesspool that is my life.

Especially when he sweeps a hand in front of his gauze choker and rasps, "I see you eyein' my pearls."

I snort. "You got me."

"Hater." Quint winces and stifles a laugh as I join him behind the counter. "So … you gonna tell me what that was all about?"

I roll my eyes and plop down on the three-by-eight-foot patch of tile that I now call home. "Nope."

The sound of a throat being cleared causes both of our heads to snap toward the doorway. I push up onto my knees just enough to see Carter entering the store, followed by a very unhappy-looking grizzly bear of a man with a very pronounced limp.

"Since you won't leave your post, I figured I'd bring you a new patient to work on." Carter beams.

"Is that why you brought me down here? Dammit, boy!" Mr. Renshaw turns to leave but wobbles on his feet and has to grab Carter's arm for stability.

"Mr. Renshaw! Stay right there!" I run to the back.

I grab a rolling desk chair from what used to be the office and push it out to the center of the store where Carter's dad is breathing heavily and wiping his brow with the back of his hand. He gives me a pained smile from somewhere behind his bushy, overgrown gray beard and then flops onto the mildewed vinyl seat with a grunt.

"Jeepers. I done told y'all, I'm fine," Mr. Renshaw gasps.

"Ah, come on, old man. Rain needs a new patient. The one she's got is boring." Carter jerks his chin in Quint's direction. Then, he leans down and whispers in his dad's ear, loud enough for everybody to hear, "And he's startin' to smell."

Carter ducks suddenly as a roll of medical tape goes whizzing past his head.

"I heard that, asshole," Quint coughs out from behind the counter.

They all burst out laughing as Carter stands and gives Quinton another smile that I know all too well. It's the same one he used to give Sophie after he teased her to the point of her smacking him.

Brotherly love.

"Glad you're feeling better, man," Carter says more seriously, walking over to the counter and reaching behind it to give Quint some kind of dude handshake/fist bump thing.

The three of us were in the same grade back in Franklin Springs, and even though Carter and Quint didn't hang out that much, they've known each other since they were kids.

"Me too." Quint's words are strangled with pain, but his voice is getting a little stronger every day.

"Would you get out of here?" I huff. "You're upsetting my patients."

Carter chuckles as he strolls toward the door. I close my eyes as he passes, catching his subtle, masculine scent.

"Hey, Carter?" I blurt out just before he leaves.

Turning back around, my best friend flashes me a Hollywood smile and points a finger gun at me. "I knew it. I knew you'd rather hang out with me than stay here with a cripple and an angry, old man."

I crack a smile—my first one in days. I don't know how he does it, but Carter has always been able to make me laugh, no matter how badly I don't want to.

"Uh, *no*." I roll my eyes. "I was just wondering where you're going."

"Relax, Rainbow Brite." Carter beams.

And my heart sinks like the *Titanic*. I know that smile too. It's one that I saw more and more of toward the end of our relationship.

Carter has a secret.

"You won't even miss me … *much*." With a wink, he disappears into the hallway, and I turn to glare at my new patient.

"He gets it from you, you know."

Mr. Renshaw chuckles and wipes the last few beads of sweat from his brow. The walk over must have really taken it out of him. As soon as his laughter fades, I can almost feel his defenses go up.

"Don't worry," I say, taking a seat on the edge of the counter a few feet away. "I'm not gonna make you show me."

Mr. Renshaw relaxes into his chair. "You ain't?"

"I already know it's broken."

His nostrils flare. "How do you s'pose that?"

"By your limp. That car accident was over a month ago. If you're still limping this badly, it means something's broken, and it's not gonna heal unless you get it set and stop hobbling around on it like you've been doing."

Mr. Renshaw's rosy cheeks go pale, confirming my suspicions.

Crap. It really is broken.

"I … I didn't think it mattered, what with the end of the world comin' and all," Mr. Renshaw grumbles through his wiry gray beard. His once-bright eyes are dull, pinched at the corners in pain and red from countless sleepless nights.

"Is that why you wouldn't let anybody see it?"

He shrugs and shifts uncomfortably in his seat. "Didn't wanna worry 'em any more than they already was."

Quint and I share a quick, sympathetic glance before I hop off the counter and cross the room.

Placing a hand on Mr. Renshaw's shoulder, I say, "Welp, the world's not ending after all, so what do you say we get you fixed up?"

He shakes his head, pulling his hurt leg a little further under the chair.

"No?"

"I 'preciate you tryin' to take care of me, Rainbow; I do. But I think it's best to just let it be."

"Why don't you let me be the judge of that?"

Not that I have any idea what I'm doing.

I glance down at his leg—I don't even touch it—and the jumpy old bastard swivels away from me in his seat with a loud, "No!" He drops his eyes with an embarrassed chuckle. "I mean … I'm fine. Thanks anyway, young lady."

I huff loud enough for him to hear me. Mama used to say that the burliest men were always the biggest babies when it came to boo-boos.

Mama.

The second her beautiful, tired, stressed-out face comes to mind, I frantically grasp at the nothingness, pulling it on like a hazmat suit right before the sadness slams into me.

Once I'm safe in my feelingless fog again, I look back down at Mr. Renshaw. His face is just as guarded as mine.

"I guess we're done here then, huh?"

His bushy eyebrows lift in surprise. "You ain't gonna argue with me?"

I shake my head and swivel his chair toward the door. Using it like a wheelchair, I roll him out into the hallway. "I know better than to argue with a Renshaw. Y'all are almost as stubborn as you are cocky."

"Hey," Mr. Renshaw snaps. "If God didn't want me to brag, he shouldn't've made me so damn pretty."

I shake my head as I roll the old man back home.

When we get to the shoe store, I'm greeted by an enthusiastic tackle hug from Sophie and a sad-eyed, *sorry about your parents* hug from Mrs. Renshaw. Both of them make me want to cry.

And also remind me why leaving the tuxedo shop is such a bad idea.

It takes almost all the energy I have to crank my mouth up into a smile. I can't remember the last time I ate … or even stood up for this long. Spots begin to dance along the edges of my vision.

"He's all yours," I say, walking backward out of the store as the room begins to tilt. "I, uh … I gotta get back to Quint. See ya later …"

Once I'm in the hallway, I tear my eyes away from their disappointed faces and head back to Savvi so fast that I'm practically jogging. I keep my gaze glued to the floor and count my steps along the way to keep my eyes and mind from wandering to dangerous places.

Ninety-one, ninety-two, ninety—

As soon as I cross the threshold into my new home, I finally look up.

And find Q staring back at me.

She's leaning against the counter with her arms folded across her chest and a look on her face that says she didn't come to say hi.

"What's up, Doc?" she deadpans.

"Hey, Q. How're you?" I cringe at the fake cheerfulness in my voice.

It's like I'm in high school all over again, cranking up my Southern accent and trying to play nice with the mean girls who are just waiting around to steal my boyfriend or snip off pieces of my ponytail when I'm not looking. Well, too bad for Q; the boy and the hair are already gone.

Like everything else.

"Just came to check on my future scout." Q tosses her dreads over one shoulder as she casts a backward glance over the counter at Quint. "Looks like you been earnin' your keep, nurse lady." Her toxic, waste-colored eyes flick back to me. "'Specially since you ain't even been takin' your share."

The accusation in her tone tells me that I did something wrong, but hell if I know what.

"I'm sorry, my share of what?" I ask as sweetly as possible.

"Don't give me that Southern belle bullshit. I'm talkin' 'bout food. You know, that shit you need to stay alive? You got a stockpile around here that you ain't tellin' me about?"

When I don't answer, her slimy gaze slides over the rest of the store. Searching. "You wanna live in *my* kingdom, Snow White, you gotta share yo' spoils, undastand?"

I nod, swallowing hard, as Q walks past the mannequin stand where my overstuffed backpack is hidden underneath. Just before she breezes past me, she stops, so close I can smell the weed smoke trapped in her hair, and runs a long fingernail down my jaw.

"By the way"—her lip curls as she digs her razor-sharp talon into the underside of my chin—"you look like shit."

I clamp my jaw shut and hold her stare. I'm not about to give this bitch the satisfaction of seeing me wince, but I'm not dumb enough to slap her away either.

I need this place too much.

Q finally drops her hand with a cackle and waltzes past me toward the door. "Bet that's why ya man left."

Rain

THE MALL IS QUIET. *Quint is resting after the best day he's had since we got here, and Lamar is sound asleep with his head on my shoulder. I should be happy. Or at least content. But I feel nothing.*

I hope it lasts.

Footsteps in the hallway approach, but I'm not afraid. I'm safe here—inside this building, behind this counter. Nothing has tried to attack, shoot at, or rape me since I arrived.

Which is exactly why I'm never, ever leaving.

When the clomp, clomp, clomp *of heavy feet enter the tuxedo shop, I expect to see Carter's mop of dark curls appear above the counter—he likes to pop in while he's doing his nightly rounds—but the face I see when I look up grabs the knife handle sticking out of my heart and twists it with invisible hands. Pain, sharp and suffocating, slices through my numbness, but I don't show it. If I flinch, if I blink, he might disappear again forever.*

Wes stares at me with that infuriatingly blank expression. The one he wears when he's thinking.

He's always thinking.

I can see him perfectly, even in the dark. Shiny brown hair, flipped up at the bottom from being tucked behind his ear. Soft green eyes hooded by strong, dark eyebrows. He shaved while he was gone. And washed his clothes. I know because the hibiscus on the shoulder of his blue Hawaiian shirt isn't blood red anymore. As my eyes slide across his broad chest, I realize that all of the flowers are different now. In fact, they're not flowers at all.

They're hooded figures on horseback.

Yellow and orange and deep, dark pink.

I sigh, and for the first time since he arrived, I allow myself to close my eyes.

"You're not really here, are you?"

He doesn't reply, and I know that when I open my eyes, he'll already be gone. Vanished like a ghost into the night. With a sigh, I look up and find Wesson Patrick Parker kneeling right in front of me.

God, he's so beautiful.

I hold my breath, afraid that he might scatter like a dandelion if I'm not careful, but … I'm not careful. I reach out with impulsive fingers and tuck his hair behind his ear. When he doesn't disappear, I exhale, letting my hand linger on his cheek.

"Why did you leave?"

Wes leans into my touch and closes his eyes. "Self-defense."

Of course. Wes's recipe for survival. Supplies, shelter, and self-defense.

"What are you defending yourself from, Wes? Nothing will hurt you here."

His eyes flick open, and I feel his jaw clench in my palm.

"The only thing that will hurt me is here," he grinds out, eyes as hard as polished jade.

"If you're talking about Carter—"

"I'm talking about you."

"Me"—I shake my head and huff out a frustrated laugh—*"hurt you? Are you serious right now? You left me, Wes. You broke my heart. You wanna talk about survival? I can't survive without my heart."*

"Bullshit," Wes snaps. *"I've been doing it since the second I walked out those doors."*

I hold his stare and my breath until my eyes water and my lungs burn.

Then, as if we both run out of patience and oxygen at the same time, we lunge for one another. His fingers dive into my hair. My hands grip the back of his neck. We erase the distance with a violent desperation, and just before our lips collide, Wes whispers my name.

"Rain … wake up."

My eyes flutter open to find a very different man blinking at me in concern. This one has eyes like warm Tennessee whiskey, not cool, mossy stones. They're friendly, not fiercely guarded, and they don't stare through me; they simply stare at me.

"Hey, sleepyhead," Carter whispers with a smile, his perfect teeth almost glowing in the dark.

"Hey," I croak, rubbing my eyes.

"You remember the plan?"

"Mmhmm." I go to stretch but stop short when I feel Lamar's head resting on my shoulder. "Can you …" I gesture toward the bag of bones slumped on top of me and roll my neck in relief when Carter gently shifts Lamar so that he's lying with his head on Quint's thigh.

"Carter?" I whisper as he helps me to my feet. "Do you still dream about the horsemen?"

He pauses, looking up and to the left as he tries to remember. "Damn. You know what? I don't think I do. Why? Are you still having the nightmares?"

I shake my head as we walk out into the hallway. "No. I still see the horsemen, but they're not scary anymore … I think they're fading away."

"That's good. Now, you can start dreaming about me again."

Carter wags his eyebrows at me, and I elbow him in the ribs.

"God, you're just as bad as your dad."

"Speaking of the old man, you sure you know what you're doing?"

I swallow. "No, but the way his foot looks like it's sticking out in the wrong direction a little bit—and the fact that he can walk on it at all—makes me think it might just be a greenstick fracture."

"And you can fix that?"

I cringe and look up at Carter. "Maybe? I saw the vet do it to our dog, Sadie, when she got hit by a car that one time."

"That was in eighth grade!"

"You got any better ideas?" I snap.

Carter shrugs. "You sure it won't just, like, heal on its own?"

I glare up at him. "It's been a month, Carter. Does it seem like it's healing on its own?"

He holds up his hands in surrender. "Okay. Damn."

"Sorry," I mumble, pulling my hoodie sleeves into my fists. "I'm just nervous."

Carter wraps a long arm around my shoulders and jerks me against his side. "You got this," he says, planting a quick kiss on the top of my head. "If you think you can fix it, you can."

I relax a little, soaking up his warmth and support like a dry sponge, but all too soon, we're at the shoe store. Carter goes in first, leading me through the web of old shoe racks by the hand.

"The girls are sleeping here," he whispers, pointing over a shelf at the clearing in the center of the store.

I look in their direction, but it's pointless. It's too dark to see anything more than a foot in front of my face.

"We put the old man in the back tonight. He snores like a damn freight train when he's been drinkin'."

"Drinking?"

Bright white teeth flash at me in the dark. Carter slows his pace and leans down to whisper in my ear, "I mighta scored a bottle of some *very* bottom-shelf tequila today. Thought it might help with the pain."

His breath is warm on my neck, his fingers are laced through mine, and even though I don't want him this close ... I need *somebody* this close. Anybody.

Carter pushes open a swinging metal door, and if I didn't know better, I'd swear a construction crew was behind it, taking a jackhammer to the concrete floor.

"Jesus Christ. How much did he drink?"

"Let's just say, this is the first time he's slept through the night since we got here."

Carter pulls a small flashlight out of his pocket to light our way. We pass a few floor-to-ceiling metal shelving units before finding Mr. Renshaw passed out diagonally across a surprisingly comfy-looking sleeping bag.

"What the hell? Y'all have sleeping bags?" I smack Carter on the arm.

He chuckles. "A couple. We packed them for our trip to Tennessee. With all of our relatives heading to my Grandma's house, we thought there was a pretty good chance that we'd end up sleeping on the floor until ... you know."

"April 23?" I roll my eyes.

"Yeah."

The air between us grows heavy as I start to think about the day he left. The gates on Fort Shit I'm Not Going to Think About Ever Again Because None of This Matters and We're All Going to Die rattle, but they hold fast. That's an outside-the-mall memory. We don't allow those out anymore.

"Come on," I whisper in the silence between snores. "Let's get this over with."

Carter and I follow the beam of his flashlight to a very unconscious James "Jimbo" Renshaw. Kneeling by his sock-covered feet—nobody goes barefoot around here—I take a deep breath and push the hem of his left pant leg up to his knee.

"Holy shit," Carter blurts. The beam of light darts across the floor and up the wall as he jerks back in response to his daddy's mangled shin.

"No, no. It's okay. Look." I gesture for Carter to shine the light back down. "See how his leg is bent right here?"

"Yeah, I fucking see it. I'll never *un*see it."

"I think his bone just kinda cracked, like this." I hold up one straight finger and then bend it a little in the middle. "It didn't break the skin, there's not a lot of bruising, and he's still able to put a little weight on it, so ..." I swallow, my mouth suddenly going dry. "So, I think he just needs that fracture reset."

"What, like, we can just pop it back into place?"

"Well, it's been a few weeks, so it probably already has a good bit of tissue growth on it ..."

"Oh my God." Carter sits down next to me and rests his elbows on his knees. The beam of light lands on a cinder-block wall about fifteen feet away. "Are you trying to tell me that we're gonna have to re-break his fucking leg?"

I give him a tiny smile that feels more like a wince. "Just a little."

I count Mr. Renshaw's snores until Carter finally responds. *Five ... six ... sev—*

"Fuck it." He throws his hands up. "It's not gonna get better if we do nothing, right?"

I nod, trying my best to seem confident when, really, the thought of what I'm about to do makes me want to puke.

"We need to make a splint to keep his leg straight while it heals."

Carter swings the flashlight across the empty warehouse. "There's nothing in here but shelves and ..." The beam lands on a haphazard stack of wooden slatted things piled up in the far corner of the room. "Pallets!"

He jumps up and disappears into the darkness. I watch the circle of light bounce across the warehouse until it reaches the pile of wooden trash. A second later, Carter's foot crashes into it like a grenade, sending splintered shards flying.

My gaze darts to Mr. Renshaw, but he doesn't even flinch from the ruckus.

I do though when I reach into my pocket and pull out a certain black pocketknife.

Not now, dammit. We are not gonna think about him now … or ever.

I slice open the toe of Mr. Renshaw's sock and slide it up to cover his calf just as Carter returns with an armful of wooden planks.

He sets the boards down and takes a step back with his hands in the air. "I can't do it. I can't fucking do it, Rain. You gotta do it."

"By myself? I don't know if I'm strong enough. There might be a lot of new bone growth to get through."

"Oh my God." Carter squeezes his eyes shut.

"Stop it!" I whisper-shout.

"It's my dad, Rain. What if it were *your* dad?" He clamps a hand over his mouth the second the words tumble out. "Fuck. I'm sorry. I'm so sorry. I didn't mean to … shit."

But I'm not looking at Carter anymore. I'm staring at the drunken, bearded, snoring, middle-aged man passed out on the floor before me, and suddenly, those outside-the-mall memories are having a real hard time staying locked up.

What if it *were* my dad?

What if it were the same unemployed, self-indulgent, depressed, angry bastard who treated my mama like a punching bag until the day he killed her?

What if?

Without another thought, I grab one of the wooden pallet slats, place it on the bent side of Mr. Renshaw's broken shin bone, and hold it in place with both hands. Then, with my teeth gritted and liquid fire in my veins, I press my foot against the bumped-out part on the opposite side and give it a good, hard shove.

"AHHHHHHH!"

I hang on to the board for dear life as Mr. Renshaw sits up and tries to jerk his leg away from me. Carter grabs his thigh and presses down to hold it in place as his dad slurs at the top of his lungs.

"BEAR DONE GOT ME, AGNES! GIT MY GUN!"

Then, his eyes roll back up in his head, and just as quickly as he came to, he passes out again, free-falling toward the concrete floor.

"Fuck!" Carter lets go of his thigh and dives with his hands out like the all-star athlete he was born to be, catching the back of his dad's head just before it splatters on the ground.

The two of us share a wide-eyed stare—him holding a head, me holding a leg—until the snoring resumes. Then, after a few deep breaths, we get to work on Mr. Renshaw's improvised splint.

Carter braces the straightened bone with four broken boards—over the sock so that he doesn't get splinters—and I carefully slide Mr. Renshaw's belt off to lash them around the middle. I take off his other sock and tie it around the top and use the drawstring from his sleeping bag to secure the bottom.

"Think it'll stay?" he whispers between snores.

"If he doesn't mess with it." I take a deep breath and blow it out, bracing my hands on the tops of my thighs. "Hey, Carter?"

"Yeah, Doc?"

"You got any more of that tequila?"

"Easy, tiger." Carter plucks the bottle from my hand as I swallow my third mouthful of what might as well be gasoline.

I wipe my mouth with the back of my hand, trying to hide my grimace as the tequila scorches its way down my throat to my empty stomach.

"God, these frogs are almost as loud as your dad."

Carter coughs out a laugh, trying not to choke as he lowers the bottle from his own lips. "For real!" He turns and glares into the fountain we're sitting on and lifts a finger to his lips, shushing the wildlife.

I giggle through my nose.

"Hey, Rain?"

"What?"

Carter sets the bottle on the floor and turns to face me, his features serious in the silvery glow from the skylights. Then, suddenly, he grabs my biceps and whisper-shouts, "BEAR DONE GOT ME, AGNES! GIT MY GUN!"

I burst out laughing, doubling over and clamping my hands over my mouth as I try not to be so damn loud. Of course, that only makes it worse. "Too soon!" I hiccup, waving one hand in surrender. "Too soon!"

"Sorry!" Carter has the best belly laugh. It's so boyish and sweet, like his face, betraying his manly, six-foot-three-inch packaging.

"For real though"—he claps a hand over my shoulder— "that was fucking badass back there. Thank you."

My laughter dies down. "Don't thank me yet. I could have made it worse, for all I know."

Carter slowly shakes his head from side to side. His hooded eyes have a hard time keeping up. "Unh-uh. You make everything better, Rainbow Brite."

"Pssh. You're drunk."

"I got somethin' for you today."

"Oh, yeah? Where'd you go anyway? You never told me."

"Every few days, Q has me take everybody's phones and shit out to my parents' car to charge 'em."

"I thought your car was busted."

"It is. Dented all to hell, right in the middle of the pileup, but it's got gas, and the engine still starts up, so ..." Carter reaches into the pocket of his basketball shorts and pulls out a shiny black device. "I charged your phone."

"Oh my God." I gasp and reach for it, turning it over in my hands like some kind of artifact from a past civilization. "Where did you find this?"

"It was in your backpack the night I found it."

103

My mood sours at the mention of that night, but Carter quickly changes the subject. "Check it out!" He taps his finger on the glass, lighting it up. The wallpaper used to be a picture of us, but after he left, I couldn't stand looking at him anymore, so I changed it back to the default screen. Now, it's just stupid blue digital swirls. "Your service even got turned back on."

I stare at the phone in my hand, racking my brain for the name of somebody I could call, but … everyone I might want to talk to either left town before April 23 or …

The screen goes black.

"Hey … you okay?" Carter gives my shoulder a little squeeze.

I nod, staring at the blank screen, but it's a lie, and Carter knows it.

So, I sigh and shake my head. "I don't have anybody to call."

"What are you, forty? You don't use a phone for calling people, silly."

Carter snatches the phone out of my hand, and I watch his face light up blue as he *tap, tap, taps* on the screen. Seconds later, the soft strumming of a ukulele drifts over the croaking of the fountain frogs as Tyler Joseph sings about a house made of gold.

"You're supposed to use it to listen to your favorite band. Duh."

I smile politely at his proud, illuminated face beaming in triumph. Carter is trying so hard to cheer me up. Now's probably not the time to tell him that Twenty One Pilots was never my favorite band.

It was *his*.

"Thanks, Carter." I take the phone from him and set it on the fountain next to me, letting it play. "That was really sweet."

He nods, and his smile slowly fades. The two of us look around as we listen to the music. He nudges a loose tile back into place with his sneaker. I pick at my hoodie sleeves. He shifts a few inches closer to me. I hold my breath until I can feel my heartbeat in my neck.

"Your hair is shorter." Carter's voice rumbles in my ear as he reaches up and slides two fingers down the front strands of my black hack job.

I flinch and pull back slightly, tucking that side behind my ear. "Yep. And yours is longer."

"Car Radio" begins to play, the electronic beat mimicking my erratic pulse as Tyler raps about being unable to distract himself from his dark thoughts.

Maybe Twenty One Pilots is my favorite band after all.

"I can't believe you're here," Carter whispers, crowding my space.

I can smell the tequila on his warm breath, and the inside of my hoodie suddenly feels like a sauna.

"I thought about you every single day, Rainbow," he slurs, leaning down to press his forehead to the side of mine. "Every single second."

I place my hand on the fountain ledge beside me to help support his weight.

"I wanted to come home to see you so bad, but I couldn't stand the thought of having to say goodbye all over again. It'd almost killed me the first time."

Carter slides a hand up the outside of my thigh, and all I can hear is the sound of blood rushing in my ears.

"I missed you so much, ba—"

The second I feel his lips graze the corner of my mouth, I grab my phone and jump up. "I'd, uh … better go check on Quint," I mumble, walking away backward. "Night, Carter!"

I turn and sprint toward the tuxedo shop as the voice coming from my fist sings about not being the person their partner used to know.

I shut the device off and shove it into my pocket.

You and me both, Tyler. You and me both.

May 2
Rain

"KNOCK, KNOCK." I PEEK my head over the empty shelves and breathe a sigh of relief when I don't see Carter. "Anybody home?"

"Rainbow!" Sophie squeals, using her whole arm to wave at me from her seat on one of the black vinyl shoe store benches.

Mrs. Renshaw's face lights up too, but her husband—who is lying flat on his back on his own bench with his splinted leg propped up on an empty shelf—won't even look at me. He throws his elbow over his eyes and grumbles something unintelligible through his wiry gray beard.

"There's my hero!" Mrs. Renshaw stands and spreads her arms, ready to pull me in for a hug as soon as I make my way through the maze of aisles.

I walk directly into her embrace but find myself gritting my teeth to get through it and pulling away sooner than usual. My reaction surprises me. I love Mrs. Renshaw.

But she's not my mother.

I don't have one of those anymore, and hugging her only reminds me of that fact.

I quickly add *Mrs. Renshaw* to my mental list of triggers to avoid at all costs.

"I can't thank you enough for taking care of my big, stubborn baby over here," Mrs. Renshaw says, casting a sideways glance over at her groaning husband. "We are so, so blessed that the Lord brought you back into our lives."

"Uh … you're welcome?" I feel my cheeks heat as I follow her gaze over to my latest victim. "But I'm not so sure *he'd* agree with you about that."

"I can hear y'all, ya know," Mr. Renshaw growls.

I smile and walk over to him. "How's my favorite patient doin'?"

"Don't come near me, devil woman."

"I brought Advil."

Mr. Renshaw props himself up on his elbows. "'Bout damn time."

I glance down at his splinted leg while I dig the bottle of painkillers out of my hoodie pocket and smile when I see that it's not too swollen.

"You probably need these more for your pounding head than your leg," I tease, dropping two little brown pills in his palm.

"That damn Mexican tequila gets me every time. Now I know why they call it Montezuma's Revenge."

I laugh, nervously glancing around as Mr. Renshaw swallows his meds. "So, did you, like, send Carter to his room as punishment or something?"

Mrs. Renshaw snorts. "Oh, he's around here somewhere."

"He went looking for yooooou," Sophie adds in a singsong voice, batting her eyelashes.

Ugh. Great.

"So …" I change the subject back to the bearded elephant in the room. "Mr. Renshaw—"

"Oh, just call me Jimbo, dammit. This ain't no time for formalities."

Somebody's grouchy. Jeez.

"Okay, *Jimbo*. I think I straightened your shin bone out, so as long as you keep it in the splint and don't put any weight on it for a few weeks, it should heal correctly."

Or at least, better than before.

Maybe.

I hope.

"A few weeks!" Mr. Renshaw plops back down on his back and throws a meaty arm over his face.

"Oh, stop bein' so darn dramatic. As bad as that wreck was, you're lucky to still be alive," Mrs. Renshaw snaps.

"Yeah, Dad," Sophie chimes in.

"I mean it, Mr.—er, Jimbo. No walking or standing on it. For at least … eight weeks."

I don't know if that's even right. I just figured, if I told him eight, he might make it at least four or five.

"I can't find her anywhere, Mom. I don't know where else to—"

All of our heads swivel toward the entrance as Carter comes stomping into the store. His frustrated gaze lands on me, and I see a glimmer of embarrassment surface in his eyes before it's quickly masked by a bright, overconfident smile.

"He still breathing?" Carter chides, glancing down at his old man.

"Yeah, but I don't think he wants to be." I smirk back, appreciating that he's keeping things light and friendly.

"Boy, yer lucky I can't walk, or I'd be kickin' yer ass right about now."

Carter snorts out a laugh, all long, dark eyelashes and floppy black curls, but as I'm watching him, I get the feeling that someone else is watching me. I turn and glance over my shoulder, thinking I'm just being paranoid, but the smitten stare of Mrs. Renshaw is definitely glued to the side of my face. She flicks her eyes from me to her son, and I swear, if her irises weren't such a dark brown, I'd be able to see big red hearts floating in them.

Ohhhh, no. No, no, no.

"Well, I'll let y'all get back to your day. Just ... let me know if you need anything," I say with a smile, speed-walking back through the haphazard rows of shelves between me and the door.

My eyes meet Carter's as I pass, and just when I think he's going to let me walk away without making it awkward, he spins on his heel and follows me out the door.

"Rain, wait!"

I don't wanna talk about it. I don't wanna talk about it. I don't wanna—

I turn around and force a smile. "What's up?"

"So, about last night ..."

Damn.

"Carter, you don't have to—"

"Do you remember what I did with my flashlight? I can't find it anywhere, and everything is kind of a blur after you went *Karate Kid* on my dad's leg." He winces and rubs his forehead. "I'm pretty sure that tequila was just rat poison with a worm floating in it."

Carter gives me a small, sheepish smile as he stuffs his hands in the pockets of his athletic shorts, and of course, I know that smile just like all the others.

Carter's giving me an out.

Gratefully, I return the favor. Cocking my head to one side, I give him a scowl. "You mean, you don't remember running down the halls, shining it in everybody's rooms last night? You were shouting something like"—I put my fist to my mouth and lower my voice—"'FBI! Hand over all your marijuana, and nobody gets hurt!'"

Carter laughs and wraps an arm around my shoulders, steering me in the opposite direction of the atrium. "Man, I turn into a damn genius when I'm drunk."

You turn into something all right.

"Where are we going?"

"To have some fun."

My feet freeze, and for the second time in as many days, I feel the urge to run away from Carter Renshaw.

I don't know what's wrong with me. People don't run away from Carter; they run toward him. Literally. They can't even help it. He's just that magnetic. His smile, those eyes, that tall and chiseled body, his cocky swagger. I was just as much of a fangirl as every other female—and some of the males—at Franklin Springs High School. The only advantage I had was that I'd found him first.

I fell in love with the boy next door *before* he became the big man on campus, but once he became the big man on campus, I got the distinct feeling that he'd outgrown the girl next door. I saw his wandering eye, the way he let the cheerleaders feel him up in the hallway. I knew he wasn't always truthful about where he was or how often he had practice. And overhearing Kimmy say that they'd made out senior year only confirmed what I'd suspected all along.

That must be what this *no feeling* is about. This is about Carter breaking my trust and leaving me behind. It's definitely *not* about a certain Hawaiian shirt–wearing, gun-toting, green-eyed loner who's out there somewhere with my heart in his pocket.

Nope. It can't be. I deleted him.

"What? You don't like fun?" Carter asks, giving me a lazy grin.

"What *kind* of fun?"

"You'll see." He starts walking again with his arm still around my shoulders, obviously expecting my feet to just magically do what he wants, like everything else.

When they don't, Carter looks down at me in shock. Nobody tells him no. Especially not his sweet, eager-to-please little girlfriend, Rainbow Williams.

But that girl, *Rainbow*, she was lying to him just as much as he was lying to her. About the music she liked, her favorite movies, how much she loved to watch sports and suck his dick. Rainbow tried to be everything he ever wanted, and he still left her behind.

So, now, all he gets is Rain.

And *No* is that bitch's middle name.

"Tell me now, or I'm not going."

Carter's dark eyebrows pull together. "Seriously?"

I respond with a glare.

"Listen, I don't know what's up with your whole … *attitude*, but … it's kinda sexy." He grins.

"Ugh!" I huff and shrug off his arm, turning and stomping off the way we came.

I make it all of two steps before his hand clamps down around my bicep, and his boyish laugh bounces off the walls.

"Simmer down, Rainbow Brite."

"Don't call me that," I snap, trying to wriggle out of his grip, but his hand is so big his fingers practically wrap around my arm twice. "Let me go!"

"If I do, will you listen to me?"

I grunt and give up the fight, crossing my arms over my chest the second he lets go. I still have my back to him, so Carter walks around and stands in front of me. He's looking at me the way he looks at Sophie when she's being a brat.

"The guys and I are gonna play hockey in the old Pottery Barn, okay?" He points over my shoulder, but I don't look. "I thought you might want to come along. You always loved coming to my games back in the day. You can be my cheerleader."

He smirks, and I want to slap it off his face.

Be his cheerleader. Puh-leez.

"I'll come but only if I get to play."

The second the words are out of my mouth, I regret them very, very much. I don't know the first thing about hockey. I'm probably gonna make a total fool out of myself, twist an ankle, and ...

Oh, whatever. None of this matters, and we're all gonna die. Right?

"*You* wanna play hockey?" he scoffs.

"You heard me." I crane my neck back to look him in the eye.

As Carter studies me, I decide that putting that puzzled look on his pretty face is worth whatever sprained ligament I'm about to suffer.

Finally, he shrugs. "Okay, but they're not gonna go easy on you."

God, if you're listening, please make them go easy on me.

We walk inside what used to be Pottery Barn, and I realize it's the first time I've ever been in one. I used to stare at the gorgeous window displays when I was a kid. Everything looked so shiny and expensive and stylish. Of course, Mama would never take me inside because she knew I'd probably break a four-hundred-dollar lamp within five seconds, but that only made my longing stronger. I told myself that the day I became a real grown-up would be the day I came here and bought the first thing that caught my eye without even looking at the price tag.

Well, here I am, and even though I'm ten years too late to do any shopping, I can still feel the spirit of every glittery picture frame and smell the essence of every scented candle that used to line these shelves. Even though they're covered in dust and water stains now, the wall-to-wall hardwood floors and white custom shelves lining the open space still feel just as luxurious as they did when I was a kid. And lucky for me, everything in the store is totally free now ... as long as you're in the market for a mildewed cardboard box, a crate of broken dishes, or a random, cracked toilet seat.

A group of runaways is gathered in the center of the store, chatting. I recognize all four guys from Q's table—the accordion player in the patched-up jean jacket, the lanky teenagers with matching bullet belts and ripped skinny jeans, and the heavyset, bearded banjo player who's wearing suspenders to keep his threadbare corduroy pants from falling off.

"Well, if it ain't The Lumineers," Carter teases as we approach the group.

All eight eyeballs land on me, and instead of widening in predatory lust—like I was used to back in Franklin Springs—they narrow in disgust. These guys look at me the way their queen looks at me—like I'm a threat, a liar, an *outsider* who needs to be disposed of as soon as she's no longer useful. On the one hand, it's kinda refreshing to have a man look at me like something other than his next victim. But, on the other hand, I also kinda need to keep living here, so it might be time for me to dust off my Student Council smile and make some new friends.

Uggggggh.

With a deep breath and dead soul, I reach way down inside and find a tiny glimmer of the girl I once was. The one who could turn into whatever she needed to be, whenever she needed to be it. Usually, what I needed to be was Carter's agreeable little trophy at school, or Mama's picture-perfect daughter at church, or Daddy's gentle voice of reason at home. But right here, right now, all I need to be is *one of them.*

I scan their clothes, shoes, and visible tattoos for *anything* we might have in common, but I can't find a damn thing. I don't have dreadlocks. I don't recognize any of the band logos on their T-shirts or jacket patches. I can't even read their terrible tattoos. And they're all just wearing busted, old black Converse and combat boots.

I glance down at my jeggings, brown hiking boots, and Franklin Springs High sweatshirt and sigh.

"What's up, man?" the banjo player asks Carter without taking his eyes off me. "I hate to break it to you, but bringing your own personal cheerleader ain't gonna help you win."

More cheerleader jokes. Awesome.

"Oh, she ain't my cheerleader." Carter glances down at me with a smirk. "She's the nurse. I brought her, so she can patch you up as soon as I get done beatin' yo' ass."

The guys all laugh and walk toward each other, meeting in the center of the deserted store to high five and slap each other on the back.

Okay, I don't get it. Carter's dressed like a quintessential jock in his basketball shorts, three-hundred-dollar limited-edition sneakers, and Nike swoosh T-shirt while these guys look like something that crawled out of a punk rock band's tour bus after it rolled down the side of a mountain. And yet, here they are, laughing and talking shit like old friends.

Oh, right. Sports. They have sports in common. And penises.

I roll my eyes and sigh even harder. I should just go. I'm way out of my element, and I obviously can't muster the appropriate amount of enthusiasm or personality needed to make new friends right now.

Or ever again probably.

"Guys, this is Rain." Carter extends his hand backward and gives me a wink over his shoulder. "She's totally in love with me."

His grin is friendly, but his words land on me like a piano. I *was* in love with him—for my whole entire life actually—but now, those feelings are just a punch line for another one of his stupid, cocky jokes.

I glare at him, feeling hurt. Feeling embarrassed. Feeling like I want to spin around and retreat to my nice, safe cave and never come back out. But then I scan the expectant faces of the four strangers staring at me, and I realize something. He made fun of them too, and they didn't storm off like little bitches. They dished it right back out. Maybe that's what friends do here. Maybe Carter is just trying to be *friends* with me.

Maybe I can play this game after all …

"Carter," I deadpan, "the only person in love with you here is *you*." I tilt my head in the direction of the banjo player. "And maybe that guy."

The bullet-belt twins look at each other and then howl in unison, slapping their knobby knees through the holes in their skintight jeans. The accordion player snickers under his breath, and the banjo player's face pales for a second before splitting into a massive grin.

Cocking his head to one side, he raises a furry eyebrow and glances at Carter. "Sweetheart," he whispers, placing a delicate hand on Carter's forearm, "I thought we agreed we weren't gonna tell nobody."

I snort through my nose as I try to keep a straight face, and the entire group bursts into laughter.

Carter shakes off the banjo player's meaty hand and introduces me to the world's finest homeless hockey team. "Rain, this is Loudmouth …"

The denim-vest-wearing accordion player drops his eyes and tips the brim of his paperboy hat at me.

"Brangelina …"

The bullet-belt twins throw me a wink and an air kiss.

"And my secret lover, Tiny Tim."

The banjo player extends his proud belly and slides his thumbs behind his suspenders.

"So …" I shift my attention to the skinny gutter punks in the middle of the lineup. "Which one of you gets to be Angelina?"

"Ooh! Me!" they both shout in unison, raising their hands.

"Dude, your name is literally Brad," the one on the left snaps at the one on the right.

"That's just semantics. I make a way better Angelina. Just look at the cleft in this chin." He tilts his face toward the light streaming in from the hallway.

"What cleft?" The guy on the right squints and leans in closer. "Oh, that little thing? Here, let me make it bigger for you."

In the blink of an eye, Not Brad cocks his fist back and lets it fly, landing a blow right in the middle of Brad's chin. Brad's head snaps back, but he recovers quickly, putting Not Brad in a headlock and giving him an uppercut to the spleen.

"It's a touchy subject," Carter whispers in my ear as the two guys wrestle to the ground.

I look up to find him inches away, a smirk on his lips and pride shining out of his honey-colored eyes. That's another smile I know by heart.

The one that means I did good.

Once upon a time, that look was everything the future Mrs. Rainbow Renshaw ever wanted. I was willing to do whatever it took to earn Carter's approval. And when I did, that look was my reward. I would commit whatever I did to memory so that I could keep doing it just to get more of that look.

Now, the only look I want to see on Carter's face is his mouth hanging open when I beat his ass in hockey.

I clap my hands together, drawing the attention of the group. "As team captain, I choose Brangelina."

It turns out that hockey is just soccer with sticks, and I played church-league soccer until middle school—when I realized that church-league soccer wasn't cool. Of course, when I played, we used an actual ball and goals with nets, not a jagged piece of broken plate and sticks fashioned from wooden pallets, but otherwise, it's not really that different. Plus, Brangelina and I kinda make a perfect team. I hang back and play goalie while they run around Carter like tornadoes with ADHD. Poor guy is pretty much on his own out there. Tiny Tim's approach to goalkeeping consists of talking shit while moving as little as possible, and Loudmouth's main priority is strictly defense. As in, defending *himself* against having to interact with the puck by all means necessary.

Carter pulls his signature basketball spin move to evade Not Brad, but I block his breakaway shot with the side of my foot. I have to use the side of my foot because the stick I'm using is just two splintery pieces of pallet nailed together, and it wouldn't stop a marble. When nobody calls me on it, I raise my worthless stick in the air triumphantly.

"Boom!" I shout at Carter, but my gloating is cut short when the top half of my homemade stick swings down and practically chops my fingers off. "Ahh!" I drop my stick and grab my hand, holding it as I bounce in place and hiss through my teeth.

"High-sticking!" Tiny Tim shouts, pointing at me like a suspect in a police lineup. "High-sticking!"

"What the hell is high-sticking?"

"High-sticking is when a player is struck by a stick that has been raised above waist-level," Loudmouth quietly recites to himself while staring at the ground.

"But I hurt *myself!*"

Carter smirks. "Sorry, babe. Rules are rules. You gotta go to the penalty box."

"Penalty box?" I swing my head from side to side. "What penalty box?"

Tiny Tim points to the mildewed cardboard box I noticed when we first walked in and grins through his grimy beard.

"You have *got* to be kidding me."

"Go on, princess." He chuckles, waving me off. "Two minutes for high-sticking. Do your time like a man."

I stick my tongue out at him as I stomp over to the soggy cube of cardboard. Loudmouth follows me with his head down, and once I'm sitting inside with my knees pulled to my chest, he adds the final touch.

He picks up the toilet seat lying on the ground next to the box, and just before the quiet little accordion player slips it over my head like a statement necklace, I notice that someone has scrawled the word *PENULTEE* on it in black permanent marker.

I glare at him, but it's pointless. His eyes are on the floor, and he's already halfway back to his safe little corner of the store.

The guys howl with laughter, and my pout lasts all of five seconds before I'm laughing right along with them.

"What's so funny?" a feline voice purrs from the entryway.

My head swivels to the left where Q is leaning against the wall, looking cool as hell with her lion's mane of dreads and her kicked-back posture, but she doesn't fool me. The intensity in her eyes and tightness in her muscles tell me that she's ready to pounce on the next gazelle that crosses her path.

In fact, she can't wait.

"The doc got a penalty for high-sticking against *herself!*" Tiny chuckles, wiping a tear from his eye.

Q raises a brow as she takes in the sight of me sitting in a cardboard box with a toilet seat around my neck before her gaze cuts back to the group. "Looks like y'all could use a third then."

"But … they're supposed to be down a player for two minutes," Tiny whines.

"Two minutes is up," Q snaps back, gliding across the room to pick up my stick.

She doesn't look at me again, but I get the message loud and clear.

I'm out when she says I'm out.

And not just in the game.

I watch from the box of shame as Brad and Carter face off in the center of the store. Q's presence seems to have shaken everybody up. They all seem so quiet and distracted. After tapping sticks with Brad, Carter easily gets the jump on him, sending the ceramic shard skidding across the hardwood, straight toward our goal. But right before it goes in, Q slams her stick—*my stick*—down on the ground sideways, blocking the entire goal with a triumphant smirk. The chunk of fine china ricochets off of it, and Carter's shoulders bunch up around his ears.

I know, if she had been anyone else, he would have laid into her for cheating, but with her being his only source of food, water, and shelter at the moment, he bites his tongue and glares at me instead.

I know, big guy. I know.

Loudmouth hustles after the broken piece of plate and sets it back in the center of the store.

"I got this," Q announces, leaving her post as goalie to take Not Brad's spot across from Carter.

Not Brad shrinks away from her the moment she gets close, but Carter holds his ground.

Placing the mangled end of his makeshift hockey stick on the ground next to the broken plate, Carter looks at Q expectantly. He's not just going to let her have this. He's still a competitor through and through, and as stupid as that might seem right now, I get it.

In this post–April 23 world, the only things you get to keep are the things you refuse to let someone else take away from you.

Carter taps his stick on the ground and lifts it a few inches in the air, waiting for Q to smack it with the end of hers—the signal that it's go time—but as usual, Q plays by her own rules. As soon as he lifts his stick off the hardwood, she whacks the ceramic puck as hard as she can, sending the shard careening directly into Tiny's portly gut. The room goes from silent to deafening as Tiny clutches his stomach with a guttural wail, and the puck falls to the floor with a heart-stopping shatter.

Q makes a show of dragging an inch-long fingernail down her tongue and using it to write the number one in the air. Then, she turns toward me, victory shining brightly in her vomit-colored eyes as she tosses her almost waist-length dreads over her shoulder.

"Take care of that," she barks, flicking her ring-adorned fingers in the direction of her latest victim. "And yo, when I said you looked like shit the other day …"

The corners of her full mouth twist into something truly evil as she stalks toward me. I try to keep my face neutral as she approaches, but when she reaches out to drag one of those talons along the edge of the toilet seat around my neck, I flinch.

"I was wrong," she coos, gripping the rim between her thumb and forefinger. A glimmer of malice flashes across her face just before she leans forward, placing her lips against my ear, and whispers the word, "Flush." Before I have time to react, she jerks her hand to the left, sending the toilet seat spinning around my neck like a horseshoe. Q throws her head back and cackles as sharp, stinging heat sears my cheeks and burns my eyes. "*Now*, you look like shit!"

She turns and sashays toward the entrance, still chuckling to herself, and Brangelina parts for her like the Red Sea. I quietly lift the toilet seat over my head and clutch it to my chest like a teddy bear. Carter squeezes Tiny Tim's shoulder while keeping his furious eyes locked on me. Loudmouth is practically rocking in the corner.

And, in that silence, we hear it.

The pounding.

Q stops for a second, listening like the rest of us, but when she spins around, it's like there's a completely different person in her place. Her face lights up, her mouth splits into a manic grin, and her wide eyes dart from person to person, scanning our expressions for signs that we hear it too.

Completely ignoring the fact that we're all glaring at her like she just stabbed our dog, Q snaps her fingers and yells, "Ohhhh shit! Y'all know what time it is?"

Tiny Tim shrugs off his anger and nods.

Loudmouth appears to be blushing.

Brangelina grins at each other and does a dramatic jump high five.

And Carter's lingering gaze heats my skin.

"It's bath time, muhfuckas!"

Rain

Q'S HUSKY VOICE GROWS more and more distant as she takes off down the hallway, yelling, "Bath time, bitches!" at the top of her lungs.

Brangelina and Loudmouth follow, no questions asked, and even Tiny Tim, with a wince and a moan, saunters off behind them.

"Hey, Tiny?" I call as I step out of the cardboard box.

He stops in the store entrance and turns toward me. Sad brown eyes, tucked inside a frame of shoulder-length dreadlocks and bushy brown facial hair, stare back.

"Come see me in the tuxedo shop later, and I'll take care of that for you." I give him a sympathetic smile and glance down at the puncture wound he's covering with his thick hand.

Tiny salutes me with two fingers before trudging off in the same direction as his friends.

Suddenly, it's just Carter and me and the sound of the rain beating down on the roof. His eyes burn like liquid gold, molten hot with unexpressed rage, and are locked on me like I'm the void he wants to pour it all into.

"You okay?" he asks, stalking across the room toward me.

"I'm fine," I snap, dusting the dirt off my ass. "Is she always that much of a bi—"

Before I can finish my insult, Carter stops a foot in front of me and claps a huge hand over my mouth.

He scans the room with wide eyes and then whispers, "In case you haven't noticed, you're the only other girl here her age. Q doesn't like competition, so I suggest you keep your mouth shut and your head down if you want to stick around."

"Ugh!" I jerk away from him and cross my arms over my chest. "So I just have to take her shit?"

Carter's jaw clenches, and his nostrils flare. "Look, I don't like it either, okay? You think it's easy for me to sit back and watch somebody disrespect my friends like that? Fuck no. But we have nowhere else to go, do we? Not unless—"

"No," I cut him off before he can say another word about places that no longer exist.

Carter closes his mouth and nods. I didn't realize there was a glimmer of hope in his eyes until it was extinguished. "Okay then. Home sweet mall it is. Come on."

He extends his hand to me, but I just stare at it.

"Where are we going?"

"To take a shower."

"Shower?"

Carter rolls his eyes. "When it rains, everybody runs up to the roof to shower off. Q has a stash of soap and shampoo and shit up there. It's"—he lifts a shoulder in a nonchalant half-shrug—"*fun*."

"Q," I spit her name out like it's a bloody, cracked tooth before something occurs to me. "Wait. So, everybody up there is ... naked?"

Carter chuckles and takes my hand even though I didn't give it to him. "Told you it was fun."

"But … what about your parents? What about Sophie?"

He starts walking backward toward the door, tugging on my hand with a playful, overconfident grin on his face. "It's not really their scene. They duck out the back door of the shoe store and shower off behind the bushes." He gives my hand a tug. "Come on, Rainbow Brite … if you're lucky, I might let you wash my back."

Suddenly, my hand is free, and my feet are moving, and my face is hot, and I can hear Carter's smug voice behind me insisting that he was, "Just kidding."

But I don't stop. I don't care about his stupid joke. I have a much, much bigger problem right now.

I run straight back to the tuxedo shop and practically scream at Lamar to take Quint up to the roof to shower off. They look at me like I have two heads, but I can't rein in my panic. The walls are closing in, and I need them to get the hell out before I have a full-blown meltdown.

"Go!" I shout, shoving a finger in the direction of the door.

Quint is finally healthy enough to maybe handle a flight of stairs.

Maybe.

I hope.

"Just don't touch his bandage!"

"Okay, *Mom*. Jesus." Lamar holds his hands up before helping his big brother off the floor.

I want so badly to rush over to them, to help Lamar get him cleaned up, but … I just … I just *can't*.

As soon as they're out the door, I lift the white cube in the center of the store that was once a pedestal for a prom-ready mannequin and pull my backpack out from underneath. I sink to the floor and dig through the contents, feeling my chest tighten more and more with every passing second. A clap of thunder shakes the walls, pushing me to move faster.

I find the travel-sized toiletries that I packed from home and have to squeeze my eyes shut and count backward from twenty to keep from picturing the beachfront motel where those little bottles came from.

... three ... two ... deep breath ... one.

Squeezing the shampoo and conditioner bottles in my fists, I focus solely on my surroundings and begin to walk backward out of the tuxedo shop entrance. Another clap of thunder makes me jump as I turn and continue to move in reverse toward the doors at the end of the hallway.

I can do this.

Step.

I don't have to look at anything.

Step.

Not that there's anything out there.

Step.

Nope.

Step.

Nothing at all.

I feel the rain spitting on the side of my face through the broken windows just before my back hits the smooth metal handle of one of the main entrance doors.

Every beat of my heart feels like a lightning strike, reverberating through my body and making me tremble. The entire hallway stretched out before me is empty, and although it's still early afternoon, the storm has darkened the mall to the point that I can't even see the fountain from here.

Good.

The darkness helps calm my nerves. It helps me lose myself and pretend.

I'm just gonna step out this door into another ... wetter *... part of the mall. That's all. I'm not going outside. There is no outside. This is the ... the ... mall shower room. Yeah.*

I set the bottles on the ground and pull off my clothes as quickly as possible, throwing them in front of me far enough that they won't land in one of the puddles forming by the door. Then, I press my naked back to the door again, cherishing the feeling of cool metal against my heated skin.

I'm in the mall. And when I push through this door, I'll still be in the mall. No big deal.

I memorize which bottle is in which hand—*shampoo right, conditioner left*—and then, with a deep breath and my eyes screwed shut, I push against the door with my body. A gust of wind blows my hair into my face, but the feeling of rain pouring down on me doesn't come. Only a slightly stronger mist, still spitting at me sideways.

The awning! Dammit!

My heart lurches into high gear as I realize that I have farther to go. Instead of walking straight back into the open parking lot to get out from under the cover, I decide that I need to stay close to the building. I need something to keep me grounded. With my knuckles against the brick and the plastic bottles in my fists, I move sideways in the direction of the mist. The droplets grow larger with every blind step I take, and when they finally begin to soak my hair and chill my skin, I stop. I can't remember which bottle is the shampoo and which is the conditioner, and I'm too terrified to open my eyes and check. So, I choose one blindly, squeeze the contents into my hand, and begin to scrub my entire body furiously.

I hear a sizzle in the air before the next clap of thunder. It's so close that it shakes the ground under my feet and elicits excited screams and nervous laughter from the people on the roof.

People on the roof.

"No!" I yell, possibly out loud, as I push the fear down and try to tell myself that I'm not outside.

The world I left and all its hurts don't exist anymore. There is no trigger out here that could possibly hurt me. But I am, and it does, and when I take one more step out from under the cover of the awning—when I feel my feet sink into something earthy and soft and as familiar as barefoot Easter egg hunts and summer games of tag—I find it.

Thunder claps, and pain seizes me like a lightning bolt striking from the ground up. The grass under my feet hurts worse than anything I thought I might encounter out here, but I've missed it so much that I can't bring myself to move.

I miss it all so fucking much.

The shampoo running down my face smells like summer vacation, and I can't stop the tears or the memories from coming now. I remember my dad taking me out into the ocean so deep that I could barely touch and showing me how to find starfish with my toes. The heartbroken look on his face when Mama said we had to throw them all back. The one he smuggled home in his suitcase that caused the entire car to smell like dead fish for months.

The memories come faster and faster, slamming into me from all sides. Now, the overgrown grass is smashed beneath my knees, my shins. Cool mud squishes between my fingers as I dig them into the soft earth, desperate for something to hold on to as the pain slices through me.

Fireworks on the Fourth of July.

S'mores around the burn barrel after raking all the fall leaves.

Christmas movies. Curling up with Mama on the couch. Slightly crooked stockings. Very burnt cookies for Santa. Catching my dad at three in the morning, wrapping presents with a cigarette hanging out of his mouth.

And then I see Wes ... beautiful, guarded, wounded Wes ... asleep in my bathtub after burying them both.

I test my legs. I have to crawl away from this nightmare. I have to get back inside. I have to get away from the smells and the textures and the sounds of this deleted world. On wobbly limbs, I claw my way back to the door and don't stop until it's firmly closed behind me.

Pressing my back to the cool metal again, I suck in as many deep, mildew-scented breaths as it takes for my heart rate to finally begin to return to normal. When I open my eyes, I expect to feel relieved. I'm back in my safe new world now. I never have to open that door again.

But the second my gaze lands on the entrance of the Hello Kitty store, that's exactly what I do.

I turn and push that sucker wide open.

So that my puke will land on the sidewalk.

May 3
Rain

A KNOCK ON THE door makes me jump, causing the brittle pages of the ancient tuxedo catalog I'm sitting on to crinkle loudly.

"Come in," I call out, but my voice doesn't want to work, possibly due to the hours I've spent sobbing in this very spot since yesterday.

I clear my throat to try again but decide not to. I don't care who's there. I don't want them to come in.

The Savvi Formalwear office door opens anyway, letting in a slice of light from the hallway. It tears across the floor, missing me by inches.

"Yo, boss lady ..." Lamar steps into the doorway. His silhouetted short, messy dreads bounce as his head swivels from left to right, scanning the dark room for signs of life. Then, he snorts out a laugh. "What the hell you doin' down there?"

I peer back at him as if I were viewing him from the grave. As if the activities of the living were beyond my grasp. Speaking. Feeling. Giving a damn. I remember doing those things. I just don't remember how I did them.

"You sittin' under the desk 'cause Mr. Renshaw took the rolly chair?" Lamar laughs. "Or was there a tornado warnin' I don't know about?"

I stare back, waiting for the words to come, but they don't.

I'm sorry. Rain's not here anymore. I cried her out. This is just her fleshy wrapper, left under a desk like a wad of chewing gum.

Lamar's smile fades as his eyes adjust to the darkness of the windowless office. When he finally gets a good look at me, he says, "Hey ... you all right?"

Flipping my hood up over my head, I turn and face the wall.

"So, uh ... Quint's feelin' a little better since gettin' cleaned up yesterday. I think I'ma try to take him to get breakfast. You wanna come?" There's a note of hope at the end of his question. "I hear they're makin' eeeeggggggs ..."

I don't respond.

I hear the air leave his lungs, taking the wind out of his sails along with it.

"C'mon, Rainy Lady," he whines. "I had to help him shower *and* feed him by myself last night."

If there were a shred of feeling left in this husk of a body, the fact that Lamar is more concerned about getting help with his brother than finding out why I spent the entire night curled up in a ball under a desk in a dark room might hurt. But it doesn't. Nothing can hurt me anymore.

I'm not even here.

"Fine. I'll do it myself. Again!"

The door slam echoes in my ears for several minutes after he leaves. Or could it be hours? I don't know anymore. I feel like I'm floating in primordial ooze. Disconnected from reality. Disconnected from my thoughts and feelings. Disconnected from time.

The only thing I can feel is my body, and the longer I sit here, the more it makes itself known. My throbbing bladder, my growling stomach, my aching legs and back—they join together in a chorus of pain until I have no choice but to move.

With everyone still at breakfast, the store is quiet. I make my way down the hall on rubbery legs. I watch them as they lift and step, but my brain doesn't register the impact. It's as if I'm wearing virtual reality goggles.

Maybe I'm going crazy.

I open the door to the employee restroom and prop it open so that I can see what I'm doing as I shimmy my jeans down and sit on the edge of the sink to pee.

When I'm done, I continue to sit there, staring at a lacy spiderweb draped over a useless air-conditioning vent, admiring the dark gray nothingness swirling inside of me. Now that my bladder's not full anymore, I am empty.

Truly and completely.

I zip and button my jeans with numb, clumsy fingers and make my way back to my cave. This time, I walk with my entire shoulder hugging the wall. I keep my gaze fixed on the entrance to the store—it's too disorienting to look at my feet—but before I make it back to the office, a demon with slime-colored eyes and a mane made of snakes fills the doorway. Her jerky gaze lands on me—or what's left of me—and a sneer splits her face from ear to ear.

I know I should be afraid of her, but that feeling is gone too. All I can do is stare back and wait for her to attack.

"There you are, *Flush.*"

She stalks toward me with the posture of a gangster even though she's wearing baggy black men's pants cut off at the knee, motorcycle boots, and a black T-shirt that's at least three sizes too big. She doesn't stop until she's standing right in front of me. Then, she yanks the hood off my head. Grabbing a handful of my hair, Q jerks me forward. I don't feel the pain. I only hear her take a long, deep breath as she lifts a fistful of my hair to her nose.

"Fresh as a fuckin' daisy." Q shoves my head backward, and her eyes blaze. "Riddle me this, bitch. How is it that you show up wit' nothin' but the clothes on yo' back, you ain't been eatin' my food, you ain't been usin' my muhfuckin' shampoo, yet here you is, alive and smellin' like a gotdamn rose bush?"

I stare at her from the safety of the nothingness and blink.

"Where's … yo' … shit?" She jams two fingers into my chest with each word, her face mere inches from mine.

"I'm sorry," I say, the sound of my own voice taking me by surprise. "Rain isn't home right now."

Q's face darkens, and her hand coils into my hair again, yanking my head down sideways.

"Rain don't have a home, bitch. This *my* home, and I'm here to collect my muhfuckin' rent." Her grip on my hair tightens to the point that I finally register the pain, and I'm almost relieved to feel it. "You got two seconds to tell me where the fuck yo' stash is before I put you *and* ya little boyfriends out."

Lifting my eyes, I glance over her shoulder at the white plaster mannequin in the center of the store. Q turns her head to follow my gaze. Then she shoves me to the ground and stomps off in that direction.

I watch from my sideways spot on the hall floor as the mannequin falls to the ground like a cut tree. The thud of it is quickly followed by the sound of a zipper and wild cackling laughter, but all I can focus on is the blank stare of the plaster man, lying in the same position as me. Expressionless. Empty. Unfazed.

Is this what I've become?

Q drags me by my hair down the hall to the food court, rambling on about Christmas coming early, but still, I feel nothing. Not when we get there and a hush falls over the crowd. Not when Carter slams his plate down and stands up with eyes full of fury. Not when Mr. Renshaw tries to do the same, only to wince and tumble back into his rolly chair with a frustrated grunt. I feel nothing when Mrs. Renshaw covers Sophie's eyes or when Lamar and Quint look on helplessly. And when Tiny, Loudmouth, and Brangelina chuckle as Q shoves me toward their table, my only thought is about Tiny's wound and how he never came by to let me take a look at it last night.

"From now on, we gon' call dis bitch muhfuckin' Santa Claus!" Q announces as she unzips my backpack and dumps the contents out in the middle of their table.

The runaways gasp and cheer and lunge for the pile, but Q slaps their hands away as she presents each item.

"Granola bars!" She holds the box up to an enthusiastic rabble from the table. "Slim Jims!"

"Yay!" The crowd cheers.

"What the fuck is dis? *GoGo squeeZ applesauce?*" She reads the label.

"Fuck yeah!"

"Band-Aids, aspirin, antihista-whatever-the-fuck." She blindly tosses each item over her shoulder, pelting me with medical supplies, before she goes completely still. "Oh, helllll nah."

Q glares at me with murderous eyes before holding up a variety box of Kotex. "Bitch, you had muhfuckin' tampons this *whole time!*"

I see a flash of movement and close my eyes just before the back of Q's hand meets my face, all four of her chunky silver rings slicing across my cheekbone.

Time stands still as pain explodes across the side of my face.

I feel like I'm on a sitcom where one of the characters is freaking out, so another character slaps them and yells, *Snap out of it!*

Well, Q's slap snaps me the fuck out of it. Only there's no laugh track. No commercial break. No lovable neighbor at the ready with a zinger of a punch line. It's just pain. And humiliation. And tears. And loss. All the feelings I've been so graciously disconnected from burst through my defenses like a tidal wave in the wake of that slap.

Once time begins to move again, I realize that the entire cafeteria has erupted into hysterics. Everyone is on their feet. Everyone is yelling. Carter has one of the runaways by his ripped T-shirt and is screaming in his face. Brad and Not Brad are hauling me to my feet, high-fiving my limp palms for taking "one helluva hit." Q is standing on the table, tossing peanut butter sandwich crackers into the crowd like dollar bills. And Lamar is scurrying around the madness, picking up the medical supplies that Q pelted me with.

Then, just as suddenly as the outburst began, it stops.

And everyone turns to face the glowing TV monitors behind the fast-food counters.

Meanwhile ...
Wes

THUMP ... THUMP ... THUMP ... SCRRRRAPE.

Fuck.

My heart begins to pound as I listen to my foster mom's boyfriend stumbling up the stairs.

Thump ... thump-thump ... WHAM.

The thin walls rattle as he careens into them, ricocheting up the stairs and down the hall like a three-hundred-pound racquetball.

"Fuck you," he mutters to no one, and I reach under my pillow to grab my knife.

Ms. Campbell went to bed hours ago, which means Limp Dick here didn't get to fight with her tonight. She's been doing that—going to bed earlier and earlier, taking enough sleeping pills to tranquilize a horse, just so that by the time he gets fuck-shit-up drunk, she'll already be passed out.

And it's been working—for her.

Slam! My door swings open so hard that the knob punches a hole in the Sheetrock wall.

I try not to flinch, but I can't help it.

I hope he didn't notice.

"Wake up, you worthlessss sack of shit."

I grip the handle of my pocketknife tighter and crack one eye open to glance at the motherfucker unfastening his belt as he lumbers toward my mattress. The hall light is on, and I notice that the peeling wallpaper just outside my open door isn't faded yellow with light-blue cornflowers on it anymore.

It's blood red with black hooded horsemen all over it. Each one is carrying a different weapon over his head as he charges—a sword, a scythe, a torch, a mace. But they don't scare me anymore.

And neither does this asshole.

Because now I know this is just a dream.

"Get up, boy!" the disgusting, sweaty, pig of a man staggering toward me yells as he slides his belt off and pulls it taut, making a snapping sound with the leather.

I close my eyes.

It's just a dream.

I'm in control.

He can't hurt me anymore.

I hold my breath and lift my pointer finger off the handle of my knife, smiling as a smooth, metal trigger magically appears beneath it.

"Ahhh!" I sit up and swing my gun out in front of me, ready to shoot the face off that sweaty, worthless piece of shit.

But no one's there.

I'm not in Ms. Campbell's foster home anymore. I'm alone, on a couch, being assaulted by the sunlight that's streaming in through a pair of dingy plastic blinds.

"Fuck," I groan, flopping back down onto the sofa and throwing my forearm over my eyes.

Even though I woke up before that motherfucker had a chance to beat the shit out of me, it feels like *somebody* did. My head throbs like it's been slammed repeatedly in a car door. My equilibrium thinks I'm on a dinghy in the middle of a hurricane. And I'm pretty sure everything inside my body has gone sour.

Hell, everything in my entire fucking *life*.

When I open my eyes again, I'm not sure what day it is or how long I've been here, but I know exactly where the fuck I am by the fading scent of death in the air.

I groan and rub my swollen lids.

From my sideways viewpoint on the couch, my eyes focus on an empty bottle of Grey Goose lying sideways on the coffee table, mirroring my miserable position.

I squeeze my eyes shut and pinch the bridge of my nose as I vaguely remember stomping through the rubble of Carter's burned-up house and pulling everything salvageable out of the still-intact freezer.

Including a handle of vodka.

My plan had been to find a new place to crash—maybe a nice, abandoned bachelor pad with a fully stocked beer fridge and a pool—but the highway was only clear maybe another block or two past Rain's house. With the riots in Franklin Springs still going strong, there was no point in risking a flat tire just to get another gun pulled on me in town by some jacked-up meth head who hadn't slept in three days.

So, I came to the one place I knew would be empty.

It had nothing to do with the fact that a certain rag doll–looking, mindfuck of a girl used to live here.

I just needed supplies and shelter.

And a shitload of vodka.

The sound of a car engine has me bolting upright again. I haven't heard a car on this road since I got here. I lean to the left so that I can see the road through the gap between the blinds and the window frame. The highway is only clear from here to the Pritchard Park exit, so whoever this is, they might be coming from the mall.

Staring into the sunlight only makes my head pound harder, but I hold my breath and squint through the pain. When the vehicle finally comes into view, I release that breath in the form of a snort. Slowing to a crawl in front of Rain's house is the motherfucking mailman. Dude doesn't even pull to a complete stop. He just throws a handful of envelopes at the mailbox lying on its side in the driveway and keeps on going.

Unbelievable.

So this is what, "You are encouraged to resume your daily lives," looks like. Bury your dead. Barricade your front doors. Scavenge for food. But hey, we got the utilities up and running again! Your bill is in the mail!

I scrub a hand down my face, feeling at least a week's worth of stubble beneath my palm, and decide to take advantage of those utilities before the county realizes the owners of this house are buried under two feet of red dirt in the backyard and cuts them off again.

I stand and wait a second for the room to stop spinning before I head for the stairs.

I spent the worst night of my life on the second floor of this house. The door on the right is where I found Mrs. Williams—or what was left of her after her husband blasted her face off. The door on the left is where I found Rain's lifeless body after she took a fistful of painkillers, lying on a mattress with a shotgun blast through it, too. And this bathroom—

I flip the light switch and wince as the fluorescent light illuminates what feels like a scene from another life.

Rain's pillow still sits on the floor by the toilet where I spent most of the night with my fingers down her throat. Her long, thick black braid is still lying on top of the trash can in the corner of the room. And vanilla-scented candles still cover every flat surface. I'd pulled them out of Rain's bedroom that night to block out the stench of death from the rest of the house, but now, I'd take blood and brains over sweet vanilla.

Because it reminds me of her.

When we first met, Rain smelled like sugar cookies, birthday cake, vanilla frosting with rainbow sprinkles—things I wished my mom had baked for me as a child, things I smelled and tasted at other kids' houses. Kids whose parents remembered their birthdays. Kids whose parents loved them.

That's what Rain smelled like to me—the kind of love I always wanted but never had.

But after a few days, she didn't smell like vanilla anymore.

She smelled like *me*.

I took every good, pure, sweet thing about Rain, chewed it up, and swallowed it.

I'm the reason she took all those pills that night.

I'm the reason she almost joined her parents in the dirt out back.

And I'm the reason she's probably lying naked in Carter's arms right now.

There's a reason none of my houses ever smelled like vanilla.

It's because love doesn't exist in my world.

I step over the pillow and turn the handle on the shower faucet as far as it will go. The pipes groan and rattle in protest, but a second later, water sprays from the faucet. I sigh and set my gun down on the counter, pushing some of the candles aside to make room. I pull off my Hawaiian shirt and lay it on the closed toilet lid. Then, I turn sideways to look at my bullet wound in the mirror. It's damn near healed.

I close my eyes and remember the way it felt when Rain put that first bandage on. Her touch was so gentle, but the pain it caused was excruciating. I'd wanted a woman to touch me like that my whole life, and once I felt it, I knew walking away would hurt worse than any fucking gunshot ever could.

I hate being right.

I blow out a shaky breath and go to strip off the rest of my clothes when the sound of voices has me reaching for my revolver.

Standing in the space between the sink and the open bathroom door, I press my back against the wall and listen. I can't make out what's being said over the sound of the shower, but I definitely hear someone downstairs.

A million different scenarios run through my mind, but the only one that makes sense is that it's pillagers snooping around for supplies. They're not gonna find much downstairs unless they check the freezer or swipe the keys to the motorcycle or truck, but the fact that they're talking at full volume despite hearing a running shower upstairs tells me that they're ballsy as fuck—and probably well-armed.

I tiptoe down the hall with my gun drawn. With each step closer to the living room I get, the clearer the voices become. The one talking right now is definitely male, which is good. I have no problem shooting the fuck out of a man. And, with another few steps, I can tell he's definitely a good ole boy. This isn't one of the Glock-toting gangbangers from the grocery store. This is one of the rifle-slinging, pickup truck–driving rednecks who tried to jump me in town.

I take the stairs as quietly as possible with my back against the wall. By the third stair, I begin to make out a few words here and there—words like *violation* and *willful disobedience*. By the fifth, I find their source—a glowing TV screen reflected in the framed poster above the couch.

I exhale and take the stairs a little less quietly the rest of the way to the living room but keep my gun drawn just in case.

"Governor Steele," a female reporter on the TV says. She's wearing so much makeup I suspect she's trying to hide the fact that she's just as hungover as I am. "Are you saying that what we're about to witness is a public trial of sorts?"

"No, ma'am," the bloated, old bastard answers, snatching the microphone out of her hand.

Turning to face the camera, Governor Steele puffs up his chest as a slow, evil smile curls up into his jowly, pockmarked cheeks. "What y'all are about to see heah ... is a public execution."

I drop to the couch and set my gun on the coffee table.

"Excuse me," the reporter says, leaning into the microphone that Governor Fuckface stole from her. "Did you say ... execution?"

"That's right, young lady. The events of April 23 have given the human race a new lease on life, and we must protect it at all costs. We were facing global extinction due to our bleeding hearts, and the only way to enshuh that never happens again is to protect the laws of natural selection *tooth and nail*." The motherfucker pounds his doughy palm with the butt of the microphone. "In the words of the late, great Dr. Martin Luther King Junyuh, 'Desperate times call for desperate meashuhs.'"

"Governor, *sir*, I believe it was Hippocrates who said—"

He yanks the microphone even farther away from the leaning reporter. "We are no longuh countries divided! We are one race—the human race—and our sworn enemy is anyone who dares to defy the laws of natural selection again! The future of our very species depends on swift ... just ... *permanent* consequences." His jowls bounce as he shakes his fist in the air.

"But, Mr. Governor—"

The balding piece of shit actually shoves the reporter back with his forearm and takes a step toward the camera. "Today, y'all will see the lengths to which your government is willing to go to protect you from evah havin' to face the possibility of extinction again. We take this responsibility very seriously, which is why anyone reported to us for engaging in activities that save or sustain the life of someone with a terminal disability, injury, or illness will be tried within forty-eight hours and, if convicted, sentenced to death."

The camera pans to the right, past the shell-shocked reporter and the gold-domed Georgia State Capitol building behind them, and swivels around to face a grassy clearing surrounded by people.

"From now on," the governor continues, walking into view, "Plaza Park will be the final resting place for those who choose to defy the laws of natural selection in the great state of Georgia!"

The crowd cheers.

They actually fucking cheer.

"Because these criminals chose to violate the laws of naychuh, their bodies will be returned to naychuh as the ultimate atonement."

At the governor's gesture, the camera tilts down, revealing a four-by-four-foot hole dug out of the earth and a sapling with roots wrapped in burlap next to it.

"A Southern live oak, the majestic state tree of Georgia, will stand where these traitors fall as a reminduh that Mother Naychuh is the true lawmakuh now, and if we disobey her again, she will feed on us all."

He pauses for dramatic effect and then barks, "Bailiff, bring out the accused."

A tall, thin man in a cop uniform parts the crowd, dragging an older, white-haired guy behind him. He's wearing a prison uniform that looks like it's made out of the same burlap material the tree roots are wrapped in. His hands are bound behind his back. His eyes are blindfolded, and his mouth is gagged. He stumbles a few times as they trudge over the uneven grass, but he appears to be coming willingly.

My already-sour stomach turns putrid as I watch the bailiff stand him directly in front of the hole, facing the governor.

No. No, no, no, no, no …

"Doctuh Macavoy, you were arrested on April 29 at Grady Memorial Hospital for allegedly continuing the use of life-support procedyuhs after being ordered by your superiors to cease all Intensive Care Unit functions. During your trial on April 30, you were found guilty of this crime, and as such, you have been sentenced to death. If you have any last words, you may speak them now or forevuh hold your peace."

The bailiff removes the burlap gag from Dr. Macavoy's mouth.

He swallows, and with trembling lips and a quivering voice, he says, "Elizabeth Ann, I … I will love you forever and always. Take care of the girls for me. Tell them not to be sad. Tell them …" He sniffles. "Tell them whenever the wind blows, that's me giving them a hug."

By the time the gunshot rings out, I'm already halfway up the stairs.

Rain

I SQUEEZE MY EYES shut and cover my ears just in time, but I can still hear the gunshot blast and *slump* of a body falling into a hole even through my hands. The image of the gentleman in the burlap jumpsuit still blazes behind my eyelids, only now he is two men, both wearing red bandanas and pointing their pistols at Wes outside of Huckabee Foods. I watch their bodies jerk from the impact of my bullets. I hear their grunts and gurgles and gasps for air all over again as they fall onto a bed of broken glass at our feet. I feel the weight of the gun in my hand and the guilt on my conscience, and suddenly, I don't know who to feel sorrier for—the executed or the executioner.

When I finally open my eyes and lower my hands, the hole is gone. In its place stands a baby oak tree—even taller than the man who stood there before it—and Governor Steele, who's posing next to it with a golden shovel that has obviously never touched a speck of dirt. With every camera flash, his grin widens, and his pose becomes more and more heroic. But when the camera pans over to the reporter for final remarks, she has none to give. She simply stares into the lens, the blank look on her face mirroring my own until the screen goes black.

I stand, slack-jawed and silent, as the gravity of what I just witnessed settles around me. But I seem to be the only one. Within seconds, the uproar in the food court picks up right where it left off. They treat the broadcast like it was just another bad reality TV show, shocking at the time but forgotten as soon as it's over.

Q goes back to pelting the crowd with supplies from my backpack, working them into a frenzy as she mimics Governor Steele. "Return to naychuh, you filthy criminals! Pow! You a tree! Pow, pow! Now you a tree too! Hey! Stop movin', muhfucka! I said, you a tree!"

I stumble backward through the mosh pit of manic runaways until I bump into the burn barrel. Then, I spin around and head straight for the hallway. I pass Carter's family, clinging to one another at their table, but I don't stop when they call my name. I don't ever want to stop. For the first time since he left, I finally understand how Wes must have felt on his way out the door.

Because for the first time since I got here, I want to leave too.

But when I try to muster the courage to lift my head, to look out those broken windows I've been avoiding instead of down at my own two feet, I watch them turn and tread into the tuxedo shop instead.

Because, as much as I want to be, I'm nothing like Wes Parker.

I'm not brave.

I'm not strong.

I'm weak and scared and possibly going crazy.

That's probably why he left. Because Wes wears his past like armor while I wear mine like chains.

I lift the mannequin back onto the white cube in the center of the store. Then, I close the cabinet doors and checkout stand drawers that Q didn't slam shut while she was hunting for my supplies. I straighten the entire store, even adjusting the mannequin stands along the sides of the room so that they're perfectly spaced and symmetrical, until I feel my blood pressure go back to normal. Until the urge to scream and pull my hair out passes. Until I feel like I have a thimbleful of control in this fucked up new world.

When the boys come back, the place looks good as new, and so does Quint ... almost.

I hop up onto the counter while Lamar dumps an armload of bandages, pills, and ointments on the dust-free surface next to me.

"Look at you, up and walkin' around. Did you get somethin' to eat?"

"Did I get somethin' to eat?" Quint winces in pain and lifts his fingertips to the bandage around his neck.

"You just got your ass handed to you by Queen Cuntface," Lamar finishes for him. "And you wanna know if he ate?"

I slam my hands over Lamar's mouth and shush him with wide, warning eyes.

Quint looks from him to the far corners of the room, as if he's searching for surveillance equipment.

"Are y'all for real?" Lamar mumbles before shoving my hands away. "I can't even call her a—"

"Shh!" Quint and I hiss in unison, waving our hands in his face.

But it's too late. Lamar's insult must have had the power to conjure Satan herself because Q waltzes in not one second later.

I slide off the counter, and Quint and I stand on either side of Lamar, as if we could actually protect him.

Her serpentine eyes slide across the three of us before settling on the boy in the middle. "Saw you and your bro here helpin' yaselves to a little breakfast this mornin'. Now, I been reeeeal patient wit' y'all, but now that I know ya girl here's been holdin' out on me, well ..." She spreads her arms wide and then slams her hands together with a loud clap. "Look at dat. My patience done run the fuck out."

"No!" I blurt out, bile and panic beginning to rise in my throat. "Please don't kick us out. Please. I ... I can't go back there. I ... we ..." My eyes swing from Quint's to Lamar's. "We don't have anywhere else to go!"

"Aww ... ain't that about a bitch? Maybe y'all shoulda thought about that before you fucked wit' ya landlord." Q's expression goes from sarcastic to murderous. "Get the fuck out."

"Please!" I cry, taking a step forward to reach for her arm.

Q yanks her arm out of my grasp before grabbing my shocked face with splayed fingers. Her thumbnail jams into my jawbone as the talons of her first two fingers stab into the swollen bags beneath my eyes, pulling my bottom lids down. She assesses me like a cat, trying to figure out if she wants to eat me now or play with me first.

"Touch me again, and I'ma take ya eyeballs and wear 'em as earrings, bitch."

I try to squeeze my eyelids shut and whisper, "I'm sorry," against her palm.

Q groans and releases my face with a shove. "I'll let y'all stay—on one condition." She turns her attention on the boys to my right and sneers, "These two lazy-ass muhfuckas start scoutin' ... *now*."

"No," I blurt and shake my head. "Please. They can't go out there. Quint still has an open wound, and Lamar ..." I turn and look at the smart-ass standing next to me. "He's just a kid."

"Boo-fuckin'-hoo, bitch." Q pretends to wipe a tear from her eye and flick it at me. "Scout or get the fuck out."

My frantic mind races through every possible choice. Even though the very thought of going outside makes me feel like the room is spinning and the walls are closing in, I can't risk getting kicked out or losing the only friends I have left.

With a heaving chest and sweating palms, I open my mouth to volunteer, but the voice that I hear isn't my own. It's deep and cool but with an edge that electrifies every cell in my body.

"I'll do it."

All four of our heads swivel toward the door, which is now filled with a presence I never thought I'd see again. His chestnut-brown hair is dark and wet. His pale green eyes are sad. Severe. His clothes are clean, his boots are muddy, and even from ten feet away, I can feel him. Hollow yet overflowing. Calm yet pulsing. Strong-willed and stubborn, yet … he's here.

He came back.

Wes's green gaze swallows me whole before he speaks again, "You still want to stay here?" His words are quiet, meant only for me.

I nod. It's a lie though. I don't want to stay here another second, but nodding is easier than admitting that something is so wrong with me that I can't even look outside without having a panic attack.

His soft gaze hardens as it settles on Q. "Then, I'll do it."

She claps her ring-adorned hands together and sashays toward Wes. Her full hips sway as if she were swinging an invisible tail. "I knew you'd be back, Surfer Boy," she coos, reaching up to pat him on the cheek.

Wes jerks his chiseled chin out of her reach, and she bursts out laughing.

"Oh, I forgot. You wanna keep us on the down-low." She casts an evil smirk at me over her shoulder before walking out the door.

Just before she disappears, Q turns to face Wes again. "You got until tomorrow to bring me some dish soap, lighter fluid, toothbrushes, deodorant, D batteries, and some gotdamn chocolate chip cookies, Surfer Boy. I ain't playin'."

Wes lifts an eyebrow at her but says nothing as she spins back around and prances away. When his gaze falls back on me, as cold and guarded as the day we met, I hold my breath.

"You're hurt." The words come out raspy and clipped after clawing their way through his clenched jaw.

I don't even know what to say to that.

Of course I'm fucking hurt. You left me. I needed you, and you left me.

But when Wes reaches out and runs a thumb over my bruised cheek, I wince and realize what he meant.

"Ugh." I turn my head away and hiss, "What do you care?"

"So, uh ..." Lamar mumbles as he and Quint tiptoe around us. "If y'all need us, we're gonna be ... avoiding the hell outta this conversation. Deuces."

He throws a peace sign up on their way out the door, and suddenly, it's just me.

And Wes.

Who is still staring at my freshly slapped cheek.

"Who did this to you?"

"It doesn't matter."

"Fucking tell me, Rain."

"Fine! You did this to me, *okay*? You. If you had been here, none of this would have happened!"

Wes drops his eyes, the lids stained purple from exhaustion.

Just like mine.

"I'm sorry." His voice is soft and sincere and makes me want to do stupid things like kiss his violet eyelids, so I turn and walk to the counter to put some space between us instead.

I sit on the dark gray surface next to the medical supplies. It's better over here. I feel like I can almost think now. Almost.

"I've never felt sorry for anything I've done before ... but I'm sorry for this." Wes's eyes lift, and the remorse I see in them is all the apology I need.

I want to run to him and kiss the pain off his face, but I can't. I'm paralyzed by his presence. All I can do is hold my breath and stare as he crosses the room like a ghost.

"I don't expect you to understand what it's like to fear something that doesn't make any sense"—Wes takes a step toward me. Then, another—"but this"—he gestures between us with the flick of a finger—"this scares the shit out of me."

Step.

"I was trying to protect myself."

Step.

"But when I saw that broadcast today ..." Wes shakes his head as the color drains from his face. "It made me realize that there's something I want to protect even more than myself."

Wes erases the gap between us with one final stride. His body comes to a stop between my dangling legs, and his palms find a home on my trembling thighs.

"I know you think you're safe here, but you're not. You taking care of Quint ... all these witnesses ..."

Wes cups my face just below my busted cheek. I close my eyes and lean into his touch even though it makes everything hurt that much worse.

"Piss off the wrong person, and they can make you disappear with one phone call, Rain."

I pull my eyes shut tighter and shake my head against his palm.

No one here would do that. Would they?

"Listen, I don't care if you hate me. I don't care how bad it hurts to see you with someone else. I don't care if you ever fucking speak to me again. I will suffer through all of that and more to make sure they don't fucking take you."

Wes slowly dips his head forward, but his lips don't land on my mouth. They fall like a feather onto the raised welt on my right cheekbone. The gesture is so gentle, so sweet, that it breaks my heart in two. I remember how Wes used to flinch and grit his teeth when I cared for his bullet wound. That's how I feel right now. His tenderness hurts, but only because it's making me realize how badly I needed it.

My eyes flutter open as a strange sense of déjà vu slithers into my veins. Panic replaces pain as I frantically search the flowers on Wes's shirt for telltale horseman silhouettes.

"Are you real?" I whisper, touching my fingertips to the orange hibiscus over his heart.

Wes drops his forehead to mine and slides a hand into the hair at the back of my head. "Are you?"

I reach for his breathtaking face with both hands, needing to kiss him, to touch him, to convince myself that this isn't just another cruel dream, but the sound of a clearing throat shatters the moment like a gunshot.

Wes's head whips around to face the entrance. Then, his hand forms a fist in my hair when he sees who our unexpected guest is.

Carter's jaw flexes and nostrils flare as he stands in the doorway, holding a green beer bottle with dandelions and wildflowers sticking out in all directions.

"I came to check on you, but"—he eyes Wes up and down with disgust before turning his disappointment back on me—"looks like you got *company*."

Something changes in his demeanor, and suddenly, he's Cocky Carter from high school, smirking as he crosses the room like he just sank a three-pointer to win the game.

Wes loosens his grip and leans against the counter, lazily rubbing the back of my neck.

Carter stops right in front of me and glances down at my split cheek. From here, I can see that he must have taken a pretty good hit during the food court scuffle too, because one side of his jaw is definitely swollen. His eyes flare behind his well-placed mask, but us getting smacked around by the runaways isn't what he came here to talk about.

"I just wanted to be the first one to tell you, happy birthday." He grins triumphantly, first at me and then at Wes, as he hands me the bouquet.

I accept it mechanically and stare at it in disbelief.

"It's May?" I ask quietly and to no one in particular.

"Yep. May 3." Carter puffs out his chest.

"I …" The flowers blur as my eyes look past them and focus on the floor. "I didn't think I was gonna have another birthday."

I blink and look up to find Carter watching Wes with smug satisfaction on his face and Wes watching me with thinly veiled concern written all over his.

"Thank you, Carter," I whisper, giving him a one-armed hug while my free hand grips Wes's bicep. "I'll see you later, okay?"

I'm sure Carter and Wes are glaring at each other over my shoulder, but Wes won't give him the satisfaction of acting like he gives a shit.

"A'ight, Rainbow Brite," he says, shooting me with a finger gun and a wink as he walks backward toward the door. "Come by later. My folks wanna tell you happy birthday too."

I don't respond, and the second Carter's six-foot-three-inch frame is out of sight, I feel Wes's whole body tense up beside me.

I set the flowers down and turn to face him.

"Please don't freak out. Carter and I are just fr—"

"It's your birthday?" Wes's eyebrows lift and pull together.

"Oh. Uh … yeah. I guess it is." I smile, still trying to process the fact that I lived to see twenty after all.

"Fuck." He tucks his damp hair behind one ear and stares out into the empty hallway. "I didn't know."

I laugh. "If it makes you feel any better, I didn't know either."

"It doesn't," Wes deadpans.

Then, without warning, he leans over and seals his lips to mine. My thoughts scatter. My heart pounds. The lights behind my closed eyelids glow brighter. And the switch in my brain that once produced joy creaks and groans until it finally breaks loose from all the rust and cobwebs and begins dumping glitter into my bloodstream again.

I touch his shoulders, his face, his hair—anything I can get my hands on that will help me believe that he's really here.

He's really here.

Wes angles his head as he deepens our kiss, attacking me with a passion I haven't felt since …

No. No, no, no.

The glitter switch turns back off.

The lights dim.

My heart sinks like a cinder block, pulling my thoughts down with it.

Breaking the seal of our mouths by no more than a quarter of an inch, Wes tells me what I already know is coming.

"I gotta go."

"But ... you just got here," I whisper, feeling the long fingers of despair beginning to wrap around my throat.

"I'll be right back. I promise." Wes gives me a determined stare and one last peck on the lips, but I'm too stunned to return it. "If I'm gonna get Q's shit while it's still light out, I gotta go now."

And, before I finish nodding, the best birthday present I ever got walks right back out the door.

Wes

"OF COURSE IT'S HER fucking birthday. Why would the day I show up empty-handed after disappearing on a weeklong bender *not* be her fucking birthday? God, I'm such a fucking asshole."

I stomp across the empty parking lot, talking to myself out loud and gesturing with my gun, not giving two shits who might see me. The only people who travel these streets anymore are Bonys and people too stupid or desperate to be afraid of them.

Looks like I just joined the second category.

The ground is wet from the storm last night, and the sky is still cloudy and gray. The wind blows my unbuttoned shirt around like a cape as I approach the intersection in front of the mall, and I like it. I like the electrical charge in the air. It feels like any-fucking-thing could happen. It feels like I could march right the fuck down this street into that pharmacy and take down anyone or anything that stands in my way.

It feels like I just kissed the shit out of Rainbow Williams.

I turn and take the sidewalk instead of going back behind the shopping center because, right now, I'm fucking invincible. Rain is still here. Nobody's called the cops on her yet for saving Quint. And she's not fucking Carter. I could tell the second that little bitch cleared his throat. If the two of them had hooked up, he would have come at me with his pop's rifle, not some smartass comment and a side-eye.

The next thing I know, I'm standing directly in front of the shattered CVS door. No wild dogs. No bloated, dreadlocked corpses. No homicidal maniacs on motorcycles.

I look to the swirling sky and give a little salute.

I guess God likes me when I'm trying not to be a piece of shit.

I knock on the metal frame of the door with the barrel of my gun. I know there's a chance some strung-out Bony is gonna blow my head off as soon as I peek inside, but I also know it's possible that the place is open for business again. The mail is running—sort of. The power's back on. Hell, Burger Palace never even fucking closed.

"Y'all open?" I call out, standing with my back against the bricks.

"Depends on how you're payin'," an apathetic adolescent voice replies.

I pull the door open and spot the Bony kid who saved my ass the last time I was here sitting behind the checkout stand, reading *Gearhead Magazine*. He's wearing a black hoodie with neon-orange skeleton stripes spray-painted on it, but it doesn't swallow him the way it did a week ago. He seems to fill it out a little better somehow, and the purple bruise around his eye has faded to a subtle greenish-yellow. I stop in the doorway when I notice that the .32 he used to blast his old man is sitting on the counter, aimed directly at me.

He lifts his eyes and does a double take as recognition wipes the apathy off his face.

"'Sup, kid?" I lift my chin.

"'Sup." His tone and expression are guarded, but he hasn't shot me yet, so that's good.

"They got you mannin' the place by yourself now?"

The kid lifts one shoulder in a half-assed shrug.

He's alone. Good.

"Listen …" I take a few steps farther into the store. "I need a few things. I'm hoping, maybe we can work something out."

The kid raises his non-bruised eyebrow. "You got weed?"

Fuck. Of course a fourteen-year-old kid is gonna want weed.

"No, but I think I know where I can get you some ammo for that .32."

I'm pretty sure Rain's dad had a small arsenal tucked away in the corners of that house. I just gotta dig a little more.

His eyebrow falls back into place, and he looks down at his magazine. "Nah. Got a full clip … except for one."

He glances back at me with hatred in his eyes, and I know exactly where that one bullet went.

"I got something else you might be interested in." I take another step closer. "I wouldn't normally offer this to a kid, but you seem like a smart guy."

I pull a bottle of hydrocodone out of my pocket and rattle the contents. I found it when I emptied Rain's dad's pockets before I buried him. I figured that bastard would have something with some street value on him.

The kid's eyes light up at the sight of that little orange bottle, and I know I got him.

"This shit's better than cash. You can get anything you want out there with this—as long as you *don't fucking eat it.*"

The little punk rolls his eyes and hands me a plastic bag from under the counter. "Three pills to fill up a shopping bag. Five, and I'll throw in a case of water."

I laugh and shake my head. "Dude, I think you and I are gonna be damn good friends."

Rain

I CAN'T BELIEVE I'M *twenty.*

> *I can't believe Wes came back!*
> *I can't believe he's gone again.*
> *I hope he's okay out there.*
> *He'll be fine. I'm the one who got beat up, and I stayed in here.*
> *Q. What a bitch.*
> *At least she's letting us stay.*
> *She's gonna make my life a living hell though.*
> *Not that it wasn't already.*
> *But now Wes is back!*
> *But what's gonna happen when he remembers how much he hates this place?*
> *He's gonna leave again, and then what?*

I'll die. I'll fucking die.

Or I could go with him.

No, I can't do that. I can't even look out the window!

Shit. He is gonna leave again, and if I'm not better by then, I'm gonna be stuck in here with Q forever.

My thoughts ping-pong back and forth in my mind as my body ping-pongs back and forth across the cracked-tile tuxedo shop floor. I've been pacing for what feels like hours. The light in the hall is starting to turn that yellowy-orange color that tells me night is coming. I can't be in here by myself in the dark. I'll go crazy ... er.

Keeping my same frantic pace, I turn my feet so that they lead me out into the hall instead of back across the room for the fifteen thousandth time.

Maybe I'll go see if there's any dinner left in the food court. That'll make Q happy. She always gets pissed when I don't eat her precious food.

As I approach the atrium, I hear her booming laughter coming at me from the opposite end of the hallway. Peeking around the fountain, I see Q leaving the food court, cackling and bumping shoulders with a few of the other runaways. I'm not ready to face her again. Not by myself and especially not if she has an audience.

She's worse when she has an audience.

Instead, I turn and haul ass down the hallway on the right. I don't care where I'm going as long as I get there before Q spots me.

I notice the shoe store up ahead and remember what Carter said about his family wanting to see me. The sound of Queen Bitch and her army of dreadlocked gutter punks echoes off the atrium walls behind me, so I turn and duck into the second to last place I want to be right now.

"Knock, knock ..." I say, faking a smile as I make my way to the center of the shoe store as quickly as possible.

Sophie hops up and runs over to me, pulling me into their makeshift living room by the hand. "Rain! You came! C'mere! C'mere! We got surprises for you!"

Her mother must have braided her hair after the rain shower. It looks perfect and probably took hours. It's interesting that Mrs. Renshaw chopped all of her own hair off but still takes the time to fix her daughter's. Sadness tugs my spirits down, but I smile anyway and let the giggly ten-year-old pull me inside.

"Oh, Rainbow!" Mrs. Renshaw gasps, immediately jumping up and launching into a gospel-worthy version of "Happy Birthday."

Carter and his dad place their playing cards facedown on the bench in between them and join in, albeit with a lot less flare, and Sophie belts out the words louder than anyone.

My cheeks feel prickly and hot as everyone in the room stands and sings to me.

When the song is over, Carter walks over to me with a smug look on his face and his arms behind his back. "Ta-da!" he says, pulling one hand out to present me with a Twinkie, still in the wrapper.

A laugh bursts out of me as I reach for the spongy, golden brick of goodness. "Oh my God, where did you find this?"

"We packed some from home when we left for Tennessee. Damn things last forever." Pulling his other hand out from behind his back, Carter holds a small pocket flashlight right above the Twinkie and aims it at the ceiling. "Make a wish." He beams.

So, I do. I close my eyes and picture a beautiful, unreadable face. Eyes as soft and green as mint ice cream with features so hard they could have been chiseled from a glacier. Then, I blow.

I hear a tiny *click*, followed by cheering, and when I open my eyes, the beam of flashlight is off, as if I'd blown it out.

"Well, aren't you clever?" I tease, unwrapping the Twinkie as an excuse to look away from Carter's cocky-ass expression.

"That's what they call me—Clever Carter."

"Uh-huh." I smirk. Taking my first bite, I moan in appreciation as dry cake and creamy frosting fill my mouth.

"Oh my God, why is dis so good?" I mumble around the delicious processed treat.

"I have something for you too!" Sophie chirps, bouncing over to me with a piece of cardboard in her hands. Swiping the flashlight from her big brother, Sophie clicks it on and shines it down on the inside of a shoebox lid. Inside, there's a drawing of a unicorn Pegasus surrounded by big, fluffy clouds and floating flowers.

"Is he shitting out a rainbow?" Carter asks, nudging Sophie with his elbow.

"Uh, no! That's her tail, stupid! The rainbow is over there!"

"Guys! Stop it!" Mrs. Renshaw snaps.

"I love it." I smile, taking the shoebox and hugging it to my chest. "Thank you, Sophie."

Sophie grins and sticks her tongue out at her brother.

"I got you something too, sweetheart." Mrs. Renshaw takes a softer tone as she reaches into the pocket of her dress. Gesturing for me to hold out my hand, she drops the item into my palm, and Sophie immediately shines the flashlight on it.

My mouth falls open. "Mrs. Renshaw—"

"Now, now. Don't you try to tell me no, child. I want you to have it."

The gold necklace in my hand glitters in the light, casting yellow flecks onto my fingertips like a tiny disco ball.

"I inherited that a few years back from my aunt Rosalyn. It's supposed to be a horseshoe, for good luck, but it always looked more like a rainbow to me." Mrs. Renshaw smiles at me with pride in her full cheeks, but I have no idea what I did to deserve it.

"Thank you so much. Really. But I can't accept this."

"Oh, pssh. You can, and you will. I don't need that old thing. I got everything I need right here."

Mrs. Renshaw glances from me to her children and then over at her husband, who is still standing. He's leaning on a display shelf with most of his weight on his good leg, but still.

"Jimbo," I yell, snapping my fingers at Carter's dad. "You'd better get off that leg right now."

Mr. Renshaw chuckles and reluctantly takes a seat. "Why are y'all givin' her all these presents when she's so damn mean to me?"

"We're givin' her all these presents *because* she's mean to you, Jimbo. Heck, a few more weeks with her around, and you might even start cleanin' up after yourself." Mrs. Renshaw wags her finger at her husband.

Carter reaches over and takes the necklace out of my hand, and I hold my breath as he unclasps it with fingers almost too large for the task.

"Woman, I do plenty around here—"

The Renshaws launch into one of their spirited fake fights as Sophie giggles in delight. No one is watching as Carter reaches out and slides the ends of his great-aunt's necklace around my neck. No one sees my discomfort as his fingers skate along my skin and disappear under my dark hair.

And when Mrs. Renshaw takes the flashlight out of her daughter's hand and shines it in her husband's face, no one notices the way I cringe and step back when Carter leans forward and whispers, "Happy birthday, Rainbow Brite. We love you. *I*—"

"What the hell are you doin', woman?"

"I just thought you might want a spotlight to go with that speech you rehearsed!"

Carter is looking at me expectantly, his hands resting on either side of my neck, as something almost imperceptible pulls my attention toward the hallway.

I turn my head slightly, staring off into the darkness of the back of the store as I listen for the sound of footsteps or voices behind me. Instead, I hear something that strikes a chord deep in my soul. A familiar tone, low and constant. Then another, in a slightly higher pitch. Then, one that bends from low to high, like a cresting wave.

"I ... I gotta go," I say, stumbling toward the sounds and out of Carter's grasp. "Thank you for the birthday party."

Carter calls after me, but I'm laser-focused on finding the source of those notes. Into the darkened hall I sprint, looking left and right until I determine that the sound is definitely coming from the atrium.

More notes float through the air. I can barely hear them from here, but they fill me with hope and dread at the same time.

Bow, bow, bow, bummmmmmm.

As I get closer to the atrium, I notice that the fountain seems to be glowing. There's a haze of amber light all around it and a scent in the air that I know by heart.

Because I picked it out myself.

Bath and Body Works Warm Vanilla Sugar candles.

Rain

THE AROMAS AND SOUNDS of home assault my senses as I fight with myself to stay in control.

Don't do this. Not now. Not here.

My chest tightens. I take deeper breaths, but the air's not getting in.

Don't panic. It's just a smell. A smell can't hurt you.

But it does. It hurts because I miss it so goddamn much.

I force myself to round the side of the fountain and come face-to-face with the only thing I want to see ... surrounded by everything that I fear.

Wes is sitting on the edge of the fountain, tuning a guitar that looks exactly like the one my dad used to play when I was a kid. My pink duffel bag—the one that Mama bought me before my first sleepaway camp—is wide open on the floor next to him, and everywhere I look, there are lit vanilla candles dotting the floor and fountain.

"Wes?" My voice comes out so screechy you would have thought I'd found him handling live cobras, not lazily tuning a guitar by candlelight.

Wesson Patrick Parker lifts his head, and for a moment, I'm suspended in the space between fear and reason. That brief moment of clarity where you're not being lied to by your emotions or manipulated by your logical mind. That tiny gap where everything moves in slow motion and you're able to see things as they really are.

And what I see is Wes looking at me with one bright, twinkling eye. His shiny brown hair has fallen in front of the other one, curling slightly at the bottom where it fits behind his ear, and his lips are parted in an easy smile. The guitar he's holding, it's just a guitar. It can't hurt me. The candles he lit, the fragrance I smell—they can't hurt me either. This beautiful person brought these thoughtful things from my house, and for a moment, I am honored and humbled and crushed by the weight of my gratitude for him.

But then Wes points to a small beige throw blanket spread out on the floor a few feet away, the one Mama and I used to snuggle under when we would watch movies on her days off from the hospital, and at the sight of it, the scent of cigarettes and hazelnut coffee smashes into me like a wrecking ball.

Clarity, gone. Gratitude, demolished.

I am fear and feelings and anguish and, and …

"I can't," I mutter, shaking my head as the breaths come faster and faster. My feet scream at me to run, but I manage to keep them rooted to the floor—my need to stay close to Wes somehow overpowering my need to escape this situation.

"You can't what? Rain, are you okay? Why don't you sit down?" He gestures to the blanket again.

"I can't!" I force the words through my gritted teeth as my hands plunge into my hair. I tug hard, trying to distract myself from one type of pain with another.

"You can't sit?" His voice is low and soothing but laced with concern.

I shake my head, still tugging, still fighting with some unknown demon for control of my body.

"Okay ..."

I hear the hollow thrum of the guitar being set aside and feel Wes's strong hands wrap around my waist. Guiding me toward him, he pulls down, gently, and my body follows his silent command. I land on his lap sideways and immediately bury my face in his warm neck.

"Can you sit *here*?" he asks, wrapping his arms around my hyperventilating body.

I nod. The weight of him soothes me like a heavy blanket. The scent of him reminds me of the present, not the past. And the utter *gravity* of him is enough to pull the panic out of my body through my pores.

I take a deep breath and am shocked when my lungs actually inflate. Then, I exhale so hard I feel dizzy.

Wes exhales too, but it doesn't sound relieved. It sounds defeated.

Letting go of me with one arm, he runs a hand through his hair. "I just keep fucking this up."

I shake my head, wanting to argue with him, but my words haven't come back yet.

"I wanted to get you something for your birthday while I was out, but then I realized that you wouldn't want anything. You don't care about *stuff*. In fact, the happiest I ever saw you was when you were climbing on the back of that motorcycle, ready to leave everything you owned behind. You didn't even know where we were going."

Wes wraps his arm back around me, and I realize that I'm not hyperventilating anymore. I'm not in my body at all. I'm lost in his words, wrapped in the rough timbre of his deep, soothing voice.

"So, I asked myself what I would have done for your birthday if April 23 had never happened. If things were normal, you know? And I don't think I would have gotten you anything. I think I would have put you on a plane and taken you to Coachella."

"Coachella?" The word tumbles from my lips as they curl into a curious smile.

"Mmhmm. It's a huge music festival in California. They have it every year in the spring. Or ... *had* it." Wes's voice trails off.

"I've heard of it. Is it fun?"

He shrugs. "Never got a chance to go. It looked fun. Everybody would get fucked up and dance around with flowers in their hair." Wes reaches for something next to him. It's a little yellow daisy he probably stole out of Carter's bouquet.

The image of him doing it makes me smile.

"I want to see you like that," he says, tucking the flower behind my ear.

"What? Dressed up like a hippie?" I tease, my cheeks tingling as his fingertips slide through my hair.

"No ... happy."

Happy.

I think about that word ... about the fact that this man wants me to feel that word. I think about the fact that this man is here at all. And then something occurs to me.

"I am."

Wes gives me the side-eye.

"Now that you're here."

"So, what was all that about?" He gestures to the place where I was standing a few minutes ago.

"I can't ..." I shake my head and try again. "I can't ... see things ... or ... smell things ..." I feel my chin begin to wobble, and the tears begin to pool, but I push through. I don't want to admit it out loud. It sounds so stupid and shameful and ridiculous, but there's a freedom building behind these words, pushing on them, begging to be let out. "I can't even touch things that remind me of home ... without ..."

"Having a meltdown?"

I drop my eyes and nod.

"And I just showed up with a duffel bag full of shit from your house." Wes pinches the bridge of his nose and shakes his head. "I'm so sorry, babe. I'll get rid of it. All of it."

"No," I snap. "Leave it. I need to …" I take a deep breath.

I need to get used to this.

I need to get over this.

I need to get better so that the next time you leave, I can leave with you.

"You sure?"

I nod, keeping my eyes screwed shut.

"Well, I can't pretend like we're at Coachella if you're sitting in my lap." Wes smirks. "Here." He moves a few candles and guides me to sit next to him on the ledge of the fountain.

Picking my dad's guitar back up, he asks if I have any requests.

"I don't know what you can play."

"I played on street corners in Rome all day, every day for two years. If I don't know it, I'll bullshit my way through it." He begins to strum absentmindedly. "What's your favorite song?"

"Uh …" I search my brain for something original. Something that feels like me. But all I come back with are Carter's favorite songs.

"Twenty One Pilots?" Wes asks.

"No," I blurt, opening my eyes to glare at Wes.

"Okay." He chuckles and holds up one hand, his other firmly wrapped around the neck of the guitar in his lap. "So, you don't know what your favorite song is?"

I shake my head.

"Challenge accepted." Wes grins, and without even looking, he shreds out a heavy metal riff that catches me off guard and makes me crack up.

"Okay, so not death metal. How about …" He plays another tune, something slower. His expert fingers bend the strings until they whine.

I tilt my head, trying to figure out where I've heard it before.

"If you don't recognize Garth, then you are definitely not a country fan. Okay, what about ..."

Duh-nuh-nuh, chicka-chicka, duh nuh-nuh ...

The opening notes of "Smells Like Teen Spirit" by Nirvana have me smiling and bobbing my head immediately.

"Actually, that doesn't help at all. Everybody loves Nirvana." Wes grins.

"What did people request the most?" I ask, wanting a little glimpse into Wes's life before the world fell apart.

I want to pretend like I'm a beautiful college student studying abroad, and he's a beautiful street musician sitting on a fountain in front of the Pantheon.

"I dunno. Whatever was popular. I can't even tell you how many times I had to play 'Call Me Maybe.'" Wes smiles. "But it was classic rock that got everybody singing—and more importantly, tipping. It didn't matter if they were young, old, rich, poor, or if they even spoke English. If I played The Beatles, The Stones, Journey, The Eagles ... I made fuckin' bank, and everybody walked away from my fountain happy."

Happy. There's that word again.

"Will you play me one?"

Wes eyes me up and down while the jukebox catalog in his head flips to the perfect song. Then, with a smirk, he says, "I got it."

Chicka duh nuh-nuh nuh-nuh, duh nuh-nuh ...

My eyes light up, and my heart overflows as he plays a simple song about an American girl raised on promises, trying to find someplace in this great, big world where she can hide from her pain.

"I love it." I smile, swallowing back the lump in my throat.

"Tom Petty." He shakes his head. "Goddamn genius."

Lifting his eyes, Wes tips his chin at something over my shoulder.

"Sup?"

My heart stops, but when I turn around, it's not Q and her crew; it's Quint and Lamar, tiptoeing toward us from the food court.

"Guess it's safe to go back into the tux shop now," Lamar jokes.

"You can hang out, if you want." Wes gestures toward the blanket on the floor that I refuse to look at. "We're just trying to figure out Rain's favorite song."

Lamar and Quint share some kind of silent brotherly communication.

Then, Lamar speaks up, "Ahh … fuck it. Ain't nothin' to do in the shop 'cept stare at this ugly motherfucker all night. We'll chill with y'all."

Quint shrugs, and Lamar helps him over to the blanket. Holding him from behind, Lamar helps Quint ease down into the sitting position without having to move his head. It makes my heart swell so much to see Lamar stepping up to help his brother that I don't even realize I'm looking at the blanket until both of them are sitting on it.

My eyes go wide as I jerk my gaze back to Wes's smug expression.

Oh, you think you're soooo smart.

Wes gives my thigh a little squeeze. Then, he turns his attention back on the Jones brothers.

"Do you guys know what Rain likes to listen to?"

"'Free Birrrrrd'!" somebody shouts from up above us. Actually, two somebodies.

My head snaps up to find Brangelina standing at the top of the broken escalator with their fists in the air. They stomp down the metal stairs and take a seat halfway down.

"No, no, no!" Not Brad shouts. "I wanna hear …" He switches to his hip-hop voice. "I did it all for the nookie!"

"What?" Brad chimes in.

"The Nookie!"

"What?"

They sing the chorus back and forth as Wes leans over and whispers in my ear, "I am not fucking playing Limp Bizkit."

I giggle as Tiny Tim comes shuffling out of a dark second-story shop, holding his banjo over his head. "Did somebody say nookie?"

"Wes is trying to figure out my favorite song," I call over to them.

"She looks like a Taylor Swift girl to me," Tiny teases, taking a seat a few rows above Brangelina.

Wes looks back at me and raises an eyebrow. "You a Swiftie?"

I shrug, but before I can give him an answer, I notice a curvy silhouette stalking into the atrium from the hallway to the left—the one I never go down—shrouded in a cloud of smoke.

"Go ahead, Surfer Boy," Q calls out, her voice slurry and slow as she snaps her fingers in our direction. "Play me some T. Swift."

Wes glances down at me with hard eyes. The sharp line of his jaw flexes in the glow of the candles.

"You want me to play nice?" he whispers. The implication is clear.

You want to keep living here, or can I be a dick?

"No," I say, his question giving me an evil idea. "I want you to play 'Mean.'"

Wes smirks. "The song?"

I nod.

"You sure?"

I nod.

"All right, but you gotta sing it."

"What? No. Wes—"

"Yes." He lifts his thumb and slides it beneath the gash on my cheek, letting me know that he knows *exactly* who put it there. "You sing it."

"But ... what if I don't know the words?"

"Everybody knows the words."

Before I can argue anymore, Wes's fingers land on the strings like he's played the song a hundred times, and the "Mean" train leaves the station. I feel my chest constrict as I glance over at Q, who is now sitting on the bottom stair of the escalator, glaring at me.

When it comes time for me to sing the first line, I choke, but Wes just plays the melody again, this time murmuring the lyrics under his breath. I almost go for it, but it's not until the third try that the words actually come out of my mouth.

They're quiet at first as I tell Q that she's a bully who enjoys picking on people weaker than her.

A little louder when I tell her that she has a voice like nails on a chalkboard.

And by the time we get to the chorus, I'm declaring—not to her, but to myself—that one day, I'm gonna leave this place, and all she's ever gonna be is mean.

"Yeeeee-haw!" Tiny calls out as he joins in on his banjo, walking down the escalator stairs and right past Q, who takes a puff from her bowl and tries to act oblivious.

Brangelina stands up, arm in arm, and sways back and forth as they help me sing the second verse about how I walk with my head down because she's always pointing out my flaws.

But it's not until Loudmouth shows up out of nowhere, jamming out on his accordion like it's a cherry-red electric guitar with flames painted on it, that I finally feel confident enough to use my full voice. It's not pretty. It's not perfect. It sure as hell wasn't good enough for the Franklin Springs First Baptist Church choir. But when I look Q in the eyes and tell her she's a pathetic liar who's gonna die alone, it sounds pretty damn good to me.

Sophie comes running up beside me and starts dancing and singing at the top of her lungs, and by the last chorus, even Wes and too-cool-for-school Lamar are singing along.

When the song is over, Tiny Tim keeps it going about two minutes too long with the world's worst and most enthusiastic banjo solo. We all burst out laughing as he holds the instrument over his head like he just played Lollapalooza.

But the sound of gunfire shuts us up real quick.

As the blast echoes through the two-story atrium, making my heart stop and my hands reach for Wes, the body of the banjo explodes, showering Tiny in splintered wood.

Q stands up, unsteady on her feet, and replaces all of our laughter with a deep, stoned chuckle of her own. "Y'all muhfuckas a buncha ... *comedians,* huh?" She swings a small black handgun around in her limp wrist, gesturing to all of us with the barrel. "Y'all a buncha rock stars now?"

She stumbles as she takes a few steps forward, a self-satisfied grin on her sleepy-eyed face. "Well, you know what rock stars eat?" A slow, evil laugh vibrates through her smiling lips. "They don't eat shit."

Her heavily lidded eyes land on Tiny, who's holding what's left of his decimated banjo and looking like he wants to cry. Walking over to him, she pokes his portly belly with the barrel of her gun and sneers, "So tomorrow, *y'all* ain't gon' eat shit."

Everyone holds their breath as Q sashays toward the hallway she came from, that slow, closed-mouth chuckle punctuating the silence as she drifts away.

Taking our joy along with her.

Wes

As soon as Q walks off, I realize how badly we just fucked up.

Not only are we on that cunt's shit list now, but we got the runaways in trouble too.

One phone call. That's all it would take for Rain to get a bullet between the eyes on live TV, and we just made a whole lotta new enemies.

Everyone scatters back to their own corners of the mall, grumbling and giving us shitty looks, while Rain sits with her hoodie-covered hands over her mouth, staring at the dark hallway that Q just disappeared into.

"Soph! What the fuck was that? Get back in here!" a deep voice echoes from down the hallway behind us. I know without looking that it belongs to that smug little shit Carter.

"Coming!" Sophie calls out. Then, she turns to Rain with big, sad eyes. "I gotta go. Carter didn't want me to come out here. Happy birthday though."

"Thanks, big girl." Rain fakes a smile and spreads her arms for a hug. "You go tell your brother he's not the boss of you." She sounds so different when she talks to kids. Stronger. More confident. She sounds like a mom.

But a good one, not the piece-of-shit version I was cursed with.

As soon as the girl is gone, Rain's posture wilts like the dying daisy I tucked behind her ear.

"Q just fired a gun like, twenty feet away from her." She shakes her head.

"She's fine."

"She's gonna go hungry tomorrow. Because of me."

"No, she's not." I cup Rain's jaw and turn her miserable, beautiful face toward mine. "Everybody here has food stashed somewhere. Nobody's gonna starve, okay?"

Rain's eyes land on the floor. "This isn't the end, Wes. Q is gonna do something else. She's gonna try to get me back for this."

"Not if you leave."

Shit.

Rain's chest rises and falls as her breathing speeds up, and I know I brought it up too soon.

"I ..." She looks around—at the blanket, at the candles, at the guitar in my hands—and I prepare to hear another, *I can't.*

But instead, Rain mumbles, "I'm not ready."

"I'm not ready."

I can work with that.

I smile and tuck my knuckle under her chin, encouraging her to lift her head. I don't know how, but I feel more fucking connection in that half-inch of contact than I've ever experienced with another person in my whole waste of a life. I feel her struggle as if it were my own, and I guess, in a way, it is. The only difference between us is that she hides from her pain.

While I run away from mine.

Rain lifts her eyelids, heavy with fat black lashes, and looks at me with a silent plea.

"You will be," I answer with more confidence than I feel.

That earns me a tiny smile.

"Plus, we can't leave right now. I haven't found your favorite song."

That earns me a bigger smile.

"You really suck at this." She grins.

"Damn, woman. Give me a chance."

Rain giggles as I stand and pull her to her feet. I grab the duffel bag and guitar but leave the candles.

Maybe I'll get lucky, and we'll burn the place down.

I turn to start walking, but Rain doesn't follow. Her eyes are locked on that goddamn blanket, and before I can stop her, she's moving toward it.

Fuck me. Here we go.

I hold my breath as she lifts it off the ground. Draping it over her arms, Rain hugs the fuzzy woven fabric to her chest like a teddy bear, and I prep for the waterworks to start. I sling the guitar over my back and get ready to drop the duffel bag, so I can catch her when her knees buckle and the hair-pulling begins.

Her face crumples as she buries her nose in the cable-knit nightmare. A tear spills over her busted cheek.

But my girl stays strong.

With a deep, steadying breath, Rain lifts her head, looks at me in utter fucking sorrow, and says, "We need something to sleep on."

There's my little survivor.

Supplies over goodbyes.

I don't make a big deal about it, but inside, I'm fist-pumping like one of those *Jersey Shore* douche bags. I'm gonna get this girl outta here by the end of the week. I know it.

I sling the guitar back around to the front as we head toward the bookstore—*our* bookstore—to break the silence. "Okay, pop quiz …"

I play the guitar line from "Hey Ya!" by OutKast and laugh when she tucks the blanket under one arm and does the *clap, clap, clap* part.

"Nice. Didn't expect you to be a hip-hop fan."

"What?" She shrugs. "Everybody knows OutKast. They're from Georgia."

"True. How 'bout this one?"

I play the intro to "Call Me Maybe" and sigh in sheer fucking delight when her nose wrinkles and her head tilts to one side.

"No? What about this one?"

I pluck the first few notes of "Sugar, We're Goin' Down" as we walk into the almost-pitch-black bookstore, and Rain calls it before I even get to the chorus.

"Oh! Fall Out Boy! I love them."

I'm glad she can't see my face right now because my smile is smug as fuck.

"Did I pass?" Rain asks as I stop at the bottom of the tree house ladder to give her a hand up.

"I think I'm the one who passed." I give her a swat on the ass as she heads up and chuckle when she yelps in surprise. "I know your song."

"Oh, really?"

When I climb in behind her, Rain is sitting, facing me with her arms folded over her chest.

For a guy who has nothing to prove, I fucking love proving myself to this girl.

I sit with my back against the wall and strum lightly as I build my case.

"Yep. You like alternative music …" I switch to a gritty rock-'n'-roll riff and pause for a second when I realize that it's one that I wrote years ago after finding an old Gibson acoustic in Foster Mom Number Nine's basement. I've never played that song for anyone before.

I shake off the significance and keep talking, "But you also like girl-power anthems ..." My notes morph into the *whoa, oh, oh, oh, oh-oh* part from "Single Ladies" by Beyoncé.

Rain laughs and does the little hand movement from the video, which only fuels my ego as I settle on a new tune. It's softer and slower and definitely sadder. I'm afraid it might be too much, considering how far she's come today, but fuck it. It's the truth, and right now, the truth—and this guitar—is all I got.

"I think you might be a Paramore girl."

I tell God he'd better fucking back me up on this one as my strumming gets louder. The simple, soulful melody is synchronized with every beat of my own bleeding heart as I open my mouth and sing the first line.

About a girl watching her daddy cry.

Rain clutches the blanket to her chest and listens as I tell her the story of a woman who's afraid to get hurt after watching her parents break each other's hearts. She tries to protect herself. She tries to avoid the pain of being left. But when she finally falls in love, she realizes that it's worth the risk.

I hope she's fucking right.

I can't really see Rain's expression in the dark, but as I let the final note fade out, I know I'm going to find tears before I even reach for her face.

"How did you do that?" She sniffles, and when she leans into my touch, I know I got her.

I shrug. "When you're in the system, you get good at figuring people out. Fast."

And when you're stuck with the same bunch of assholes your whole life, like Rain, I guess you get good at hiding.

She inhales deeply and sighs. "So, what's the name of my new favorite song?"

I place the guitar in the corner and crawl over to her. Laying her down, I take the wadded-up blanket out of her arms and set it behind her head like a pillow. "'The Only Exception.'"

Gazing down at her, I know now that that's *exactly* what she is for me. The only exception to all of my rules.

No getting attached.

Leave before you get left.

Supplies. Shelter. Self-defense.

Survival above all else.

Now, they've all been crossed out with a giant X, and next to them, in murderous block letters, are the words *Protect Rainbow Williams*. That's all I fucking care about now. Keeping her safe. Keeping her—period.

I was afraid she would hurt me, but while I was gone, I realized that she's the only fucking thing in my life that *doesn't* hurt.

"Wes?" she asks, her voice small and shaky as she slides her fingers into my hair and pushes it away from my face. "Will you still be here when I wake up?"

Guilt seizes my heart and squeezes it in its fucking fist. Bracing myself on my forearms, I lower myself onto her soft, warm body and press my lips to hers. Blood explodes through my veins on contact, but I don't move. I hold that kiss until I feel her relax beneath me. Until I know she'll believe me when I finally promise, "Forever."

Satisfied, Rain pulls my face back down to hers and kisses me like forever might actually exist. Slowly. Sweetly. Without the ticking clock of April 23 looming over our heads or the hooded horsemen from hell breathing down our necks. Without blood on our hands or ash in our hair. Without wonder or worry about how it will end. Because we started at the fucking end.

Now, we get to begin.

Tilting my head, I deepen our kiss and try not to smile when I feel Rain's hips rock against me in response. We might have forever, but I have a week's worth of pleasure to make up to this woman, and I think she's waited long enough.

Gripping her hip with my right hand, I press myself against her and feel a moan vibrate through her chest.

"I missed you," she whispers, weaving her fingers deeper into my hair.

"I …" I squeeze my eyes shut, forcing myself to speak around the knot of remorse in my throat, "I didn't think you would. No one ever has, so … I'm sorry. I'm so fucking sorry, Rain. If you want me, I'm yours."

"Forever," she repeats.

My promise sounds more like a prayer coming from her lips, so I dip my head lower and seal it with a kiss. Our bodies move instinctively as I pour my heart out through my mouth—kissing her deep and slow, like a love song.

And somehow, Rain knows all the words.

Her body rolls and writhes beneath me as our tongues swirl and our breathing becomes heavy. I grind against her faster, wanting to make her come just like this—with nothing more than a kiss and promise.

"Wes," she rasps, tilting her head back.

"Mmhmm …" I hum, sucking on her fat bottom lip.

"Wes …" Rain's voice sounds more frantic, but her hips keep working in tempo with mine. "These are my only panties!"

I chuckle against her panting mouth. "Not anymore. I grabbed you some extra clothes while I was at your house."

With that, Rain grabs my head and crushes her mouth to mine. The arch of her body underneath me, the needy moan in the back of her throat as she comes undone, the way she forgave me with open arms and is holding my face right now like I'm fucking precious—it overwhelms me, and suddenly, Rain isn't the only one who's going to come from a single kiss.

I push myself off of her, kneeling between her legs to try to calm down, but the sight of Rain basking in post-orgasmic bliss before me does nothing for my throbbing cock.

Opening her eyes, Rain takes one look at my face and then lets her gaze slide down my fully clothed body to the massive bulge right in front of her. With a swollen-lipped smirk, she reaches up and unfastens my belt.

I grab her wrist in warning. "Let me make you feel good a few more times first. I have a lot of making up to do."

"It's my birthday," she says with a devilish grin. "I can do whatever I want."

Can't argue with that logic.

I let go of her wrist and watch as Rain slowly unbuttons my jeans and spreads the fly open. Her fingers slide up the shaft of my swollen cock through my boxers, and it jerks against the waistband.

Fuuuuck, this girl is killing me.

Without sitting up, Rain shimmies my pants and boxers down over my ass and licks her lips as my cock falls free.

"Come down here," she says, her voice laced with need.

I don't understand what she means until Rain grabs my hips and tugs forward gently.

Oh shit.

"You want me to fuck your mouth?"

Even in the dark, I can see Rain's skin flush at my words. She drops her eyes and nods with a tight-lipped smile.

My balls tighten, and I do as she said, straddling her waist and leaning forward onto my hands. I drop my head and watch as her kiss-swollen lips part, and her little pink tongue slides across the head of my cock.

"Fuck," I hiss, trying to hold still as she wraps her warm mouth around me and sucks her way to the end.

"Rain, you don't have to—" I start, but I can't finish my sentence because if she doesn't keep doing what she's doing right now, I'll fucking die.

I hold my breath, afraid that if I move a single muscle, I'll hurt her, but once Rain sets a rhythm with her mouth and her hands, I'm powerless. My hips buck as she takes me deeper, works me faster, sucks me harder. Sweat rolls down my neck as I struggle to maintain control, but when she moans, throaty and raw, when I hear how fucking turned on she is, I lose control.

My entire body goes rigid as I pour myself into Rain's soft, warm mouth. Waves of pleasure roll down my spine as her tongue works me over, sucking and swallowing every last drop until I'm spent and empty and full at the same time.

Rain looks up at me with a smirk on her plump lips and pride in her pretty blue eyes.

"You're fucking up my apology." I smirk back.

Rain's mouth spreads into a full-on grin. "Sorry."

"Liar." I move backward down the length of her body until I'm straddling her thighs. "Now I gotta start all over."

Rain giggles as I pull her hoodie and tank top off over her head, and the sound is music to my fucking ears. She arches her back so that I can unfasten her bra, and the smooth curves of her body are a siren's song that I can't ignore. My fingers slide over her full tits, squeezing and rolling her perky pink nipples until her hips lift off the ground in need.

Fuck.

Even in the dark, Rainbow Williams is sexier than anything I've ever seen in the light.

She reaches for my open shirt, attempting to push it over my shoulders, so I shrug it off for her along with my holster. As I pull my tank top off over my head, I feel her gentle hand slide down and around my already-hard cock.

"Uh-uh," I tease, grabbing her hand and pinning it next to her head. "Not yet."

The side of Rain's mouth curls up, and my dick jerks in response, remembering how fucking good it felt to be in there.

"You can grab this." I place her hand on her boob and give it a little squeeze, earning me a giggle. "You can grab this." I lift her hand to the top of my head, where she gives my hair a tug. "Or you can grab this." I lace my fingers between hers and feel a sudden bolt of electricity binding us together the moment our palms meet. "Got it?"

Rain nods, but the humor is gone from her face. Tender, doe-eyed sweetness replaces it as she brings our joined hands to her lips and plants a kiss on one of my scarred, busted knuckles.

Something clicks inside my heart. I feel it, like a fresh battery being snapped into place, and I realize that the aching, echoing hole in my chest—the one I've lived with my whole fucking life—wasn't there because I was empty.

It was there so that Rain could reach in and fix me.

I press our joined hands to the plywood above her head and kiss her again, this time with all my working parts. This woman found me broken and made me whole, and I'm suddenly determined to do the same for her. I will get her the fuck out of here. I will give her a happy life, even in this shithole, lawless, dumpster fire of a world, and starting right now, I will love her the same way she loves me.

As if forever really exists.

Trailing wet kisses across her jaw and down her neck, I take my time, savoring the salt on her skin and the swell of her blood pumping beneath it. When I get to her nipple, I work it slowly, with my tongue, my lips, my teeth. I time my movements with the rise and fall of her perfect, heaving tits. But when I go to pull my hand away so that I can unfasten her jeans, Rain refuses to let go. I smile against her heated skin and pull our entwined fingers down together. Clumsily, I get her pants unbuttoned and fumble to untie her bootlaces with my one free hand.

But I don't mind. If Rain wants to hold my hand for the rest of her life, I'll fucking cut it off and give it to her.

Once I slide her jeans and ruined panties off over her bare feet, Rain parts her legs for me, and it feels like I'm being welcomed home.

With our hands still joined, I kiss my way from the inside of her ankle, up to her knee—which must be ticklish because it jerks and smacks me in the fucking mouth, causing Rain to giggle—and down to the soft, needy, glistening place that I plan on worshipping for the next few hours.

When I slide my tongue up her seam and around her clit, I do it only because I want to make her feel good. There's no pretense. No impatient foreplay so that I can get off and go to bed. I don't go straight for the spots I know will make her thighs tremble and her back arch just to speed things up. I settle in, and I let her body tell me what it wants. Long licks elicit hushed moans and slow body rolls. Swirling circles earn me short whimpers. A teasing finger causes her to buck her hips against my face, but two fingers, knuckles deep, have her head thrown back and her fist in my hair. Up and around, up and around, my tongue and my fingers ride the wave of her body, rising and falling with her quickening breaths. But still, I wait. I keep her in heaven as long as I can until her fist tightens in my hair and her thighs clamp around my ears and the first flutters of an orgasm tickle my fingers.

Then, I suck.

Rain's entire body contracts around me as she writhes and pants and growls the sexiest fucking sounds I've ever heard. I slide my fingers out and replace them with my tongue, wanting to drink every drop of her the way she did me.

"Fuck, Wes," Rain rasps, pulling my face up toward her with her free hand.

Her other one is still clutching mine, and the sight of our fingers entwined has my newly repaired heart acting like it's on the fucking fritz already. It skips a few beats entirely as I climb up her boneless, spent body and press a kiss to her love-drunk lips.

"I'm not done yet," I promise, sliding my aching cock over her slippery, swollen flesh.

Rain shoves her toes into the waistband of my jeans and pushes them as far down my legs as they will go.

"I'm gonna make you come once for every night that I was gone."

Rain's head falls back onto the plywood with a dramatic *thunk*, but her hips rise to meet mine, thrust for thrust.

I would chuckle at her mixed signals, but this feels too fucking good. I drop my forehead to hers as we move with and against each other, seeking friction in the slippery mess we've made. Our mouths collide in a torrent of tongues and teeth as the pace quickens until I can't fucking take it anymore. I need to be inside Rainbow Williams more than I need my next fucking breath.

Pulling her knee up to my ribs, I surge forward, filling her completely in one delicious fucking motion.

And Rain comes on contact.

Her nails dig into my back, and her moans echo down my throat as she pulses and arches and glows in my arms.

And I follow her into the light.

The darkness behind my eyelids goes white as I hold her shuttering body to mine. As I fill her with everything that I have. Everything that I am. Everything that I want to be for her. I could stay here like this forever, basking in the afterglow of my girl on fire.

But I can't.

Because I promised this woman six more orgasms.

And from now on, I'm a man of my word.

May 4
Rain

WHEN I WAKE UP, I feel as though I've been turned inside out. The pain I used to carry around in my mind and in my soul is now only in my back from sleeping on a plywood floor. My muscles, which used to feel restless from lying around all day, are now deliciously sore. And my heart—which, just yesterday, felt like a rotting, blackened organ oozing poison into my bloodstream—now feels ripe and red where it pitter-pats against Wes's side.

It feels happy. *I* feel happy.

I bury my smile in his bare chest and tighten my arm around his ribs. His presence feels like a miracle. Like a gift from God. Some people get new shoes or fancy cars or the latest iPhone for their birthdays. I got a whole person. *My* person.

And also, like, a dozen orgasms.

Wes stretches and turns in my arms, pressing his morning *situation* against my hip as he pulls me closer.

"No horsemen last night," he grumbles sleepily, kissing my forehead.

"None at all?"

"Hmm-mm." He shakes his head as much as he can with his lips still on my face. "You?"

I try to remember what I dreamed about and smile when it finally comes to me. "Me either. I dreamed that I was in outer space. I was stranded on this tiny planet, or maybe it was just an asteroid. I don't know how I got there, but I couldn't get home. I could see Earth, but every time I jumped off the rock and tried to swim to it, I would only get so far before the little planet's gravity would pull me back down. I was so frustrated. I started to panic."

Wes pulls me closer and rests his chin on the top of my head.

"Then, all of a sudden, this rocket came whizzing through the air. It looked like the Looping Starship ride at Six Flags. There was no roof, and everybody was screaming and laughing with their arms in the air. I waved for help, but they shouted at me that the ride was full. They were just gonna leave me there, but right before the ride passed me by, you leaned out as far as you could and pulled me in. You let me sit in your lap because all the seats were taken, and you wrapped your arms around me so that I wouldn't fall out."

I kiss Wes's warm chest and feel my skin prickle with a million tingling goose bumps.

"It was the best dream I've had in a long, long time."

Wes swells even more against my hip, but he ignores it and smooths a hand over my hair. "I would go to outer fucking space to get you."

I smile.

"But I would *never* let those motherfuckers ride on my spaceship. They can all burn in hell."

I laugh with my whole body … until it makes me realize how badly I need to pee.

"Wes, I gotta go," I huff, pushing on his chest.

"Nuh-uh," he groans, pulling me closer.

"No, Wes. I gotta *go*."

Catching my meaning, he releases me with a chuckle and sits up. "I'll come outside with you."

"No, it's fine. I'll be right back," I mutter, trying to pull my hoodie and jeans on as quickly as possible.

Wes slips his holster on, throws his Hawaiian shirt on over it—leaving it unbuttoned so that his chest is on full display—and slides his boxers on over his still-hard cock. "Nah, I'm ready. Let's go."

"Like that?" I giggle, glancing down.

"What?" Wes follows my gaze to see the head of his dick staring back up at him. "It'll calm down when the cold air hits it." He shrugs.

"Wes," I hesitate. "I don't go out there … anymore."

"Oh, you found a new spot?" he mumbles, buttoning his shirt to cover the issue. "Smart. That front entrance is pretty exposed."

"No …" I sigh, already hearing the shakiness return to my voice.

Wes's head snaps up, and suddenly, he's the Ice King again. Cold. Guarded. Quietly raging and highly alert.

"What happened?" he snaps.

"Nothing. I just—"

"Bullshit. What happened?"

"Ugh! I can't think when you get like this!"

"You don't need to think. You need to tell me what the fuck happened."

"I had a panic attack, okay?" I shout. "I touched the grass, and I just … I freaked out. I can't see the trees because they remind me of home. I can't look at the highway because it reminds me of home. I can't leave this damn building because

191

everything out there triggers a memory, and memories trigger the pain, and the pain triggers the panic because if I can't shut it down immediately, it's so big and so awful that I think it might kill me, *okay?*"

I take a huge breath and blow it out through my lips as Wes studies me with unaffected eyes.

"No," he finally says, his mouth set in a hard line.

"No?"

Wes shakes his head. "No. It's not fucking *okay*. Get your shoes on. We're going outside."

"Watch your step."

I grip Wes's bicep harder as I step down off the curb and into the street.

At least, I assume it's the street.

"How're you doing?" he asks.

"I ... uh ..." I check in with myself and realize that I'm actually kind of okay.

With Wes's tank top tied around my head, I can't see anything. All I can hear is his voice. And with my boots on, the only thing I can feel is the pavement beneath my feet and his body touching mine.

I hate it when he's right.

"I'm ... *fine*, I guess."

Wes chuckles. "It's a good thing nobody's out here because you don't look fine. You look like you're being fucking kidnapped."

"Wouldn't be the first time you kidnapped me," I joke. "Besides, you're too pretty to be a kidnapper. It defeats the purpose if girls go with you willingly."

"Hold up," Wes says, stopping to bend over and pick something up.

I hear a familiar metal rattle but can't figure out what it is.

"So, you think I'm pretty, huh?" Wes asks as we start walking again. I can hear the smirk in his voice.

"Boy, you know you're pretty. Don't go fishin' for compliments."

"Nah." Wes snorts. "I'm ugly wrapped in a pretty package. But *you* ..." The deep rasp in his voice vibrates all the way down my spine as Wes leans in and presses his lips to my temple. "You're the most beautiful fucking thing I've ever seen." I feel his fingertip slide down the bridge of my nose and over my mouth and chin as if he's admiring my profile. Then, it continues lower, stopping right between my breasts. "Even in here."

I blush, grateful for the blindfold so that I don't have to drop my eyes in embarrassment.

"Step up."

I do as he said and feel the asphalt turn to soft earth beneath my feet. A few feet later, he pulls me to a stop and turns me so that I'm facing something that blocks out the sun.

"We're here. You can take your blindfold off but only look straight ahead, okay?"

"Wes, I ... I'm scared."

"I'm right here. You wanna sleep in a bed again someday? You wanna take a hot shower and eat food that wasn't cooked over a metal barrel?"

I nod, feeling my heart rate skyrocket.

"Well, this is the first step, baby. Take off your blindfold."

I take a deep breath, drawing as much strength from him as I can. I lost my mama and daddy. Wes lost his mom and sister. I was left behind by my boyfriend. Wes was rejected by thirteen different foster families. I dealt with mean girls at school. Wes was the new kid at half a dozen high schools. If he can stand out here and be ready for whatever happens next, then maybe I can too.

Sliding the ribbed tank top off my head, I bring it to my nose and inhale. The scent of Wes overpowers all my other senses, making me feel happy.

Making me feel brave.

I crack open my eyelids, letting in a tiny sliver of my surroundings, before I open them the rest of the way in surprise. We're standing two feet in front of the faded green PRITCHARD PARK MALL exit sign next to the highway.

Wes wraps a firm hand around my jaw, holding it straight. "Don't look anywhere but here, okay?"

"Okay," I reply, too curious to be afraid.

I hear the metallic rattle again and smile when it gets louder and faster.

"I noticed this can of spray paint on the ground the other day, and it made me think of you." Wes chuckles, shaking the can in his hand.

"Why me?" I smile.

"Oh, I dunno. Maybe because of the *Welcome to Fucklin Springs* sign in front of your house?"

I grin. "Shartwell Park is my personal favorite."

"So, you admit that you're a vandal?"

"I prefer the term *wordsmith*." I smirk, accepting the can of neon-orange spray paint in Wes's outstretched hand.

"See, take this sign." I pop the cap off with an experienced thumb. "A vandal would just draw a coupla dicks on it and move on." I cross out the *P* in Pritchard and easily turn the *R* into a letter *B*.

I can feel Wes grinning, but I'm too nervous to look over at him. Instead, I focus all my attention on the green-and-white—and now, neon-orange—sign in front of me.

"But not me." I give the can a few more shakes and cover the *RD* with two big, bold *S*s.

"*Bitchass Park Mall*," Wes reads aloud with pride. "I didn't even think to add the double *S*s at the end. Nice."

I turn and give him a little curtsy, but when I open my eyes, I not only see Wes; I see the entire mangled pileup behind him.

Quint and Lamar's daddy's bulldozer is a charred hunk of metal. The pavement around it, scorched and black. The tractor trailer on its side looks like a T-Rex took a bite out of it, and all around, pushed to the sides of the road, are the totaled and abandoned vehicles Quint cleared trying to get us through the pileup. I picture him lying on the pavement with that shard of glass sticking out of his neck. I picture Lamar, dazed and in shock with blood trickling into his eye from his lacerated eyebrow. I remember the sound of the explosion and the way twisted metal and broken glass rained down around us like confetti.

And then, I remember the way the inside of my mama's helmet smelled when I put it on.

Like hazelnut coffee.

Like *her*.

The scene in front of me goes blurry as the memories line up along the edges of my mind, ready to march in one by one to destroy me. The first one charges, and it's a doozy.

Christmas morning.

The last Christmas before April 23, I came downstairs to find Daddy passed out next to a puddle of his own vomit on the floor in front of the Christmas tree. Mama and I left him there while we opened presents. She brewed her coffee extra strong that morning. Made me some too. I don't know what else she put in that cup, but it made me feel warm and silly. We curled up under her blanket on the couch and watched *Christmas Vacation* on repeat until Daddy came to. It wasn't so fun after that.

"Hey," Wes says, blocking the sides of my face with his hands like blinders. "Stay with me."

I blink, pulling myself out of my head as his beautiful face comes into view.

"You did it." He beams, and the pride in his eyes is enough to make tears form in mine. "You're outside, fucking shit up like a little punk."

Wes jerks his thumb in the direction of the sign, and two warm streams slide down my cheeks as I turn to look at it. Not because I'm afraid to be out here.

But because I'm so incredibly thankful to be.

"I love you," I whisper, shifting my gaze back to the man who, just yesterday, I thought I'd never see again. "I love you so—"

Before I can finish my declaration, Wes silences me with his mouth. He blocks out the world with his hands over my ears, clutching my face as he kisses me hard. He chases the memories away with his tongue and lips and hips and smell. And I am plunged back into my favorite place.

The one where Wes and I are alone together.

A car horn breaks into my consciousness, causing me to go rigid in Wes's arms. I don't look, afraid of what I might find, but Wes does, and what he sees makes him grin against my lips. He lets go of me to salute something over my shoulder, so I give in to my curiosity and take a peek.

A small white mail truck comes puttering up next to us, and Eddie—the same mail carrier we've had since I was a kid—gives us a little wave before flipping a U-turn and heading back down the highway toward Franklin Springs.

"The mail is running?" I ask in shock.

"Sort of." Wes chuckles, lifting his tank top to re-cover my eyes. "C'mon. Let's head back. I'm starving."

"But Q isn't feeding us today," I remind him as he ties the white cotton in a knot behind my head, grateful that he's not going to push me to walk all the way back, unblindfolded.

"I told you, I have plenty of food." Wes presses a kiss to my unsuspecting lips, which part in a silent gasp as his hand slides between my legs. "That's not what I'm hungry for."

I feel so much better on the way back. Bolder. Braver. I lace my fingers between Wes's and swing our hands back and forth as we head down the exit ramp. The bright May sun warms the top of my head, and I suddenly want to feel it everywhere—on my cheeks, on my shoulders. I crave it like oxygen.

Once we're at the bottom of the ramp, I pull Wes to a stop next to the chain-link fence encircling the mall and yank my hoodie off over my head. His makeshift blindfold comes off in the process, and I freeze, both from the delicious warmth on my skin and from the war being waged inside my head.

"Rain?"

I think I can do it. I think I can open my eyes and be okay. With Wes beside me and the sun on my face, I feel like I could fly if I really wanted to.

I listen for anything that might sound … I don't know … triggering, but all I hear is the faint rumble of an engine in the distance.

Make that several engines.

"Shit," Wes spits, tightening his grip on my hand.

"Wes?"

"Bonys."

My eyes snap open and jerk in the direction of the break in the fence and then back up the ramp the way we came.

"We gotta run for it," Wes growls.

"It's too far!"

"Now, Rain!"

"No! Just … just … just put this on!" I take the can of spray paint in his hand and swap it out with my oversize Franklin Springs High sweatshirt.

Wes glances over my shoulder toward the sound of the rumble, but he doesn't argue. He yanks the hoodie on over his head in the time it takes to suck in one more steadying breath. It fits him perfectly, hugging his broad chest and shoulders, and I get to work, spraying neon-orange ribs across the front and back. Wes flips the hood over his head and pulls it down low to cover his eyes.

Tossing the empty can over the barbed wire, I stand with my back against the fence and pull Wes in front of me so that I'm mostly hidden from view.

"Kiss me!" I beg as five shiny street bikes crest the hill at the end of the street. "Like I don't want it!"

Wes doesn't hesitate, grabbing me by the throat and shoving his thigh between my legs. He angles his back toward the oncoming threat as he plunges his tongue into my mouth, and as much as I want to sag against the fence and let him, I have to pretend to fight him off.

I don't bother screaming—they won't hear me over the roar of those engines—but I make a show of shoving his immoveable chest and trying to push off the fence with my boot as he holds me in place. Wes rips my tank top halfway down the front and grabs my breast as the first motorcycle passes.

And, against my better judgment, I look.

The crew of madmen seems to move in slow motion as they take in the show. Their once-chromed-out choppers and slick black street bikes have been spray-painted with neon skulls and bones and bloody, flaming body parts just like the leather jackets and hoodies they wear. Each man has on a helmet or mask more terrifying than the one before it. Mohawked, blood-spattered, Day-Glo skulls eye us up and down as they drive by—machetes, nail-filled baseball bats, and sawed-off shotguns at the ready.

They sneer at me as I scream—for real this time—shoving Wes off of me just enough to break out into a full-on sprint.

Satisfied with our performance, the Bonys take off down the road as Wes chases after me, catching me by the wrist and spinning me around in his arms. He kisses me as furiously as he did the day I pulled him out of the Renshaws' burning farmhouse.

I might know all of Carter's smiles, but I'm quickly learning all of Wes's kisses.

This is his post-near-death-experience kiss.

I hate this kiss.

I hate the Bonys.

I hate this new world.

But mostly, I hate how good the sun feels on my skin right now because, once we go back inside, I'm pretty sure I'm never going to feel it again.

May 5
Wes

"BAILIFF, BRING OUT THE accused!"

Governor Fuckface is turning into more and more of a glorified game show host with every broadcast. He sweeps his ham hock of an arm out to gesture toward the five convicts being ushered out of the capitol building—each one bound, gagged, and wrapped in a matching burlap jumpsuit—as if he were Vanna White, revealing today's grand prize on *Wheel of Fortune.*

I shovel a forkful of eggs into my mouth and wash it down with boiled rainwater as I watch them parade the guilty past the bloodsucking saplings that have already been planted. There must have been another execution while we were out yesterday because now there are three baby oak trees growing in Plaza Park.

In a few minutes, it will be eight.

Rain pushes the food around on her plate next to me as they read out the crimes of the accused. A few more hospital workers who refused to remove life support, a woman who continued tube-feeding her disabled husband, and a mother who saved her child's life with an EpiPen after he had an allergic reaction to a bee sting.

These are considered high crimes now, but murder and rape are totally legal.

Go fucking figure.

Just before the first of the accused gets to say her last words, I turn and cup my hands over Rain's ears. She's not watching the broadcast—her gaze has been glued to her untouched breakfast ever since it came on—but I know she's listening.

Her big blue eyes lift, and for a moment, it feels like we're the only two people in the room.

Bam!

I force a small smile as the sound of a body landing at the bottom of a dirt hole reverberates through my fucking soul.

Bam!

I smooth my thumbs over her cheekbones, being extra careful with the right side, which is now sporting a gnarly green-and-purple bruise.

Bam!

The third convict takes a bullet between the eyes as Rain drinks me in with hers. The corners of her full pink lips twitch as if she wanted to smile back, but she pulls them down and drops her gaze instead.

Bam!

I can't say that I blame her. I'm probably the only motherfucker who can smile while people are being executed on live TV.

Bam!

Because I'm the only motherfucker who gets to look at her while it happens.

Across from us, Quint pushes his plate away and cups a hand over his mouth in disgust while Lamar stares blankly at the screen as if he were just watching another bad horror flick.

I pull Rain's head against my chest, thankful that she's not freaking out, thankful that she's here with me instead of lying in the bottom of a dirt hole in Plaza Park, and I begin to get the feeling that the executions aren't the only thing people are watching in the food court.

I glance up and find Carter's parents staring at us from a few tables away. His sister is wearing headphones and playing on someone's cell phone—no doubt to protect her from the mass murders happening on live TV—but her folks are none too happy. Mrs. Renshaw has the Southern decency to look away, but Carter's dad holds my stare for what feels like hours. There's no challenge in his puffy, bloodshot eyes—the old bastard can hardly walk—just a deep sadness.

I know that feeling. I've lost her before too.

Carter didn't come to breakfast with them, and honestly, I don't fucking blame him. Just the *idea* of seeing Rain with someone else was enough to make me pack my shit and go. I want to feel bad for the guy, and I would, if he deserved my sympathy. But I know assholes like him. Popular. Good-looking. Entitled as fuck. Guys like that don't take rejection well. They throw tantrums like fucking toddlers when shit doesn't go their way. And wherever Carter is right now, my guess is that he's plotting his next move, not licking his wounds.

I look around the room, taking a mental headcount, and a sinking feeling slithers into my gut.

The runaways are all accounted for at Q's table—watching their phones and smoking weed and aiming guns at each other's heads like they're Governor Fuckface on TV. Quint—who is now down to a large Band-Aid and a couple of aspirin a day—and Lamar are in a heated debate about whether they should steal a Jeep and find a place in the mountains or steal a convertible and try to find a beach house to squat in. And the Renshaws are huddled together as usual, all except for Carter.

He's the only one unaccounted for.

Until that motherfucker marches into the food court, carrying my duffel bag.

Carter shoots me an *eat shit* look as he heads straight toward Q's table, and I laugh—I actually fucking laugh—and shake my head.

So predictable.

Rain doesn't think it's funny though. She stiffens in my arms the second she sees him.

I want to reassure her that it's going to be fine. That no matter what happens, I won't let these dramatic little bitches hurt her. But I can't.

This is post-April 23.

All bets are off.

Carter stops directly in front of Q, commanding the attention of everyone in the food court, as he unzips my duffel bag and dumps it out on her table. Extra clothes for Rain, water bottles, trail mix, canned stew, dried fruit, beef jerky—all the shit I brought from Rain's house, plus all the nonperishables I've been hoarding from my trips to CVS—tumble out like bombs. The cans hit the table and roll to the floor in a series of loud clangs and bangs, and everybody holds their breath and waits for Q to drop a bomb of her own.

Her mouth curls up on one side as she admires both the spoils and the show. "Well, well, well ... what do we have here, mall cop? You tryin' to buy a spot at the big-boy table?"

"This is Wes's bag!" Carter declares in his best Captain America voice. The authority in his tone has me rolling my eyes.

Fucker would have made a great mall cop.

"He's been hiding food, supplies, even bullets!" Carter turns and aims an accusing finger directly at me. "Kick. Him. Out."

It's an Oscar-worthy performance. I'll give him that.

Q cackles. It starts low and deep, only in her throat. Then, it builds into something loud and psychotic. Suddenly, food and clothes go flying as she comes across the table, grabbing Carter by the face and kissing the shit out of him. He pushes her off and stumbles backward as she stands in the middle of the table, towering over him.

"You wanna act like a little bitch? I'ma treat you like a little bitch."

"What the fuck?" Carter yells.

His mom gasps and covers Sophie's ears even though she's too engrossed in whatever she's watching to know what's going on.

"You think just 'cause I ride ya dick whenever I want that you can tell me what the fuck to do in *my* muhfuckin' castle?" Q drops to her feet directly in front of Carter and shoves a sharp fingernail into his chest. "You ain't shit, mall cop. If I should kick anybody out, it's yo' ass. *That* muhfucka's the best scout I eva had ..." Q looks directly at me as her lip curls into a sneer, and her hips gyrate back and forth. "And he looks like he could eat the hell outta some pussy, too."

The word *pussy* is the match that detonates the powder keg. Loud metal scrapes echo all around us as a dozen chairs are pushed out at once. Carter's parents stand in disgust. The runaways leap to their feet to cheer on the madness. And I shove away from the table because Carter is stalking toward me with his hands balled into fists. I want to tell Rain to get the fuck out of here, but I don't have a chance. I'm too busy preparing for Carter to take a swing.

Which leaves her wide open for him to grab instead.

Carter wraps his long fingers around her biceps and crouches down so that they're eye-to-eye. "Rainbow, please. Just let me explain. It meant nothing, I swear!"

Rain grunts and tries to jerk away from him, but Carter doesn't let her go. He shakes her. He fucking shakes her, and her wide eyes asking me for help are the last thing I see before the darkness takes over.

The sound of Rain screaming is what filters in through my consciousness first. I blink—one, two, three times—and find myself kneeling on the ground. A mound of bloody flesh is gasping beneath me, spitting blood and teeth like a human volcano. I leap off of him and try to open my hands to reach for Rain, wherever she is, but my fists feel like they've been run through a meat grinder. There is more screaming as Mrs. Renshaw and Sophie drop to their knees beside the mangled man on the ground.

I watch their tears fall in slow motion, wondering if my bloody fists are the reason they're crying, just before I hear Rain cry out, "Noooo!"

My head snaps in the direction of her voice a split second before her tiny body collides with mine, sending us both tumbling to the floor. The wall-rattling blast of a hunting rifle being fired indoors has me back on my feet and running, dragging Rain by the hand along with me. I don't have to look behind us to know who fired the gun.

If somebody beat the shit out of my kid, I'd try to kill him too.

We pass the fountain without any other shots being fired and are in the home stretch toward the main entrance when Rain digs in her heels like we're about to run off the edge of a cliff.

"Wes, what are you doing?" Her voice is shrill and terrified, and I know that I'm not done fighting yet.

I turn and level her with a commanding stare, my eyes shifting between her and the fountain every other second. "We have to leave. Now."

"We can't!"

"Goddamn it, Rain! Either you can run or I can fucking carry you, but we have to leave right the fuck now!"

Both of our heads jerk up as we hear the *stomp, slide, stomp, slide* of Mr. Renshaw's limp coming down the hallway.

"So help me God, boy, if I catch you round here again, I'ma hang yer head on the wall like a twelve-point buck."

The metallic clank of a rifle being cocked sends us both into motion again. I shove open the heavy exit door and pull my girl into the blinding spring sunlight. Instead of hauling ass straight across the parking lot, I head for the closest parked car, using it as a barricade until I'm sure the coast is clear. Rain is breathing heavily beside me, and I can't tell if it's from exertion or panic, but I don't stop to find out.

I do what I do best.

I fucking run.

Rain

CARTER'S FACE. I CAN'T get the image of Carter's pulverized face out of my mind. The last time I saw a face that bloody …

I gasp and choke on a sob as the image of my mother lying in bed, never to wake up again, slams into my consciousness like a linebacker. It doesn't flicker, and it doesn't flash. It blocks out my vision like a gruesome bumper sticker over my eyes as Wes drags me up the exit ramp and into the woods. I count backward in my mind. I shake my head from side to side. I use my free hand to yank on my hair, but nothing's working.

We stop running. Wes is talking to me, but I can't hear him. I'm too busy trying to think of something else. Anything else. I open my eyes as wide as I can, looking all around us for a distraction, but everything reminds me of her. The woods, her motorcycle, the air in my lungs. It all reminds me that I'm alive and she's not. Wes straddles the bike, his mouth moving like he's giving me instructions, but I just blink at him. At his perfect face. Carter had a perfect face too, but Wes broke it. He broke it, just like my dad broke my mama's face. Made it ugly and bloody and gone.

Wes guides me to sit on the motorcycle. I let him manipulate my body like a rag doll.

Is this what the Paramore girl sang about? Watching your parents destroy each other just to fall in love and make the same mistake? Will Wes do the same thing to me one day?

I watch him as he picks up Mama's helmet. He shoves his wild hair behind one ear, black lashes fanning out across high cheekbones, and I know she's right. I *am* destined to make the same mistake. Because just like my mama, I've fallen madly in love with a man who is capable of doing terrible things with the best of intentions.

Wes's pale green eyes lift to mine, swimming with remorse and sharpened by fear, and I'm so lost in them that I don't realize what's happening until I'm being plunged into a dark, hazelnut-scented prison.

Wes starts the bike, and I hold on for dear life as grief wraps its powerful tentacles around me and drags me under. I can't hide from it anymore. I can't fight it off. I have no distractions. Nowhere to go. It's just me and this smell and this loss and this pain and this road taking me right back to my own personal hell.

I squeeze my eyes shut and press my forehead to Wes's back as a strangled cry fills my helmet. It is long and loud and primal and overdue.

I don't want to go back there. I don't want to go back there. I don't want to go back there. Please, God. Please don't let him take me back there.

I rock in my seat and repeat the mantra, finding some relief in the mindless repetition, but when the bike eventually begins to slow, a fresh wave of fear washes over me.

No, no, no, no, no, no, no.

I'm afraid to look up. Afraid to let go. Afraid to face the place that holds all of my best and worst memories. I'm not ready. It's too soon.

When the bike pulls to a stop, Wes turns and lifts the helmet off my head. I suck in a breath that doesn't smell like hazelnut coffee and exhale with my whole body.

"Fuck, Rain ..." Wes whispers, brushing the matted black strands away from my swollen, wet cheeks.

I keep my eyes shut tight, content to sit here and let him touch me as long as we don't have to go inside. "I'm not ready," I mumble. It's the only explanation I can give him before my face crumples again.

"I know. I wanted to give you more time, but ... time's never really been our fuckin' friend, has it?"

I shake my head, my eyes still glued shut.

"Do you think you could sit on the porch?"

I nod, not because I believe that I can, but because I *want* to believe that I can.

Wes guides me off the bike and walks me down the driveway and over to the front steps. My pulse speeds up with every step we take closer to my own living nightmare, but I push myself to keep walking.

It's just the porch. It's fine. It's just the porch.

Wes helps me sit on the top stair and then plops down behind me so that my entire shaking body is enveloped by his.

"You know how I brought all that stuff from your house when I came back?"

I nod and listen, eager for him to keep talking. Wes's voice is my favorite sound—deep and rough yet calm and quiet—and the way his chest rumbles against my back when he speaks helps me feel calmer, too.

"I stayed here while I was gone. That whole fucking time. I don't know if I told you that. Mostly, I just got drunk and felt sorry for myself, but when I wasn't passed out, I fixed the place up a little."

"Wait. You did what?" Without thinking, I turn in his arms and open my eyes.

Wes's lips pull into a sweet, boyish smile, and he shrugs. "I knew you'd come home eventually, and I didn't want you to have to see … *all that* … again. I found some paint in the garage. Got rid of the, um … *damaged* furniture. Pulled up the carpet. Did you know you got hardwoods under there?"

I shake my head and laugh as my face wars with itself over whether to grin like a lunatic or cry like one.

So, I give up and do both. I laugh and cry and look into the eyes of a man who destroys beautiful things … but who also makes destroyed things beautiful again. For me.

Then, I notice something over his shoulder.

"Wes … is that a new front door?"

His smile spreads into a grin as he turns and looks at the country-blue slab of wood behind him with the big brass door knocker. "Look familiar?"

"Yeah, it does actually. But I don't—oh my God."

Wes chuckles and turns to face me. "The front half of Carter's house only got smoke damage, so I was able to salvage a few things. It doesn't exactly match the rest of the house, but at least it doesn't have a broken-out window in the middle of it."

Wes shifts his weight and pulls something out of his pocket. Taking my hand, he drops a single key into my palm. "Found this under Carter's doormat. Welcome home, Rain."

I stare at the tarnished metal, which suddenly feels as though it weighs as much as a house.

No, as much as a *home*.

"Listen, you don't ever have to go back in there if you don't want to. We can live in the fucking tree hou—"

My heart explodes as I dive for his mouth, planting a kiss on his perfect, parted lips. I don't care if I'm ready. I don't care if he's fucked up. I don't care if we're destined to break each other's hearts. No one has ever loved me like this, and Paramore was right.

That's worth the risk.

I pull away, clutching the key—still warm from Wes's pocket—like a single rose. "I wanna see."

Wes's eyes widen as his pupils dart back and forth between mine. "You sure?"

I nod, not sure at all, but wanting to be … for him. And for me.

"Come on," I say, using his broad shoulders to help me stand. "Show me what you've done with the place."

"Rain, you don't have to do this."

I shake my head and try to put on a brave face. "I want to."

With a single dip of his chin, Wes takes a step back, clearing my path to the front door.

But it doesn't feel like a door. It feels like I'm standing in front of a massive wooden drawbridge, and inside, banging against the surface and rattling the heavy chains, is everything I've been trying to keep locked away in my mind. Every trauma. Every fear. Every bittersweet, fading memory. I was afraid if I let them out, they would trample me, but as I slide the key into the lock with shaking fingers, the rattling goes quiet. When I turn the knob and give it a push, the door opens without so much as a squeak. And when Wes reaches in beside me and flicks the light switch by the door, all those gruesome beasts I expected to find have been replaced with glittering, golden butterflies.

The living room is wide open and full of light. Instead of stained, matted carpet, shiny hardwood the color of Coca-Cola is spread out before us. The only furniture in the room is a couch and a love seat, a coffee table, and the TV stand. The walls are light beige again instead of tobacco yellow. And when I inhale, I smell fresh paint instead of cigarettes and coffee.

"Wes … I …"

"Oh shit. Hang on …" Wes darts inside and grabs an empty liquor bottle off the coffee table. Holding it behind his back, he turns to face me, an innocent mixture of pride and shame on his handsome face.

"You did all this in a week?"

"Yeah ..." Wes looks around for a place to stash the bottle. He sets it down next to the TV stand, where I can't see it. "It turns out that ripping up carpet feels a hell of a lot better than putting your fist through a wall."

Wes starts walking back toward me, but I don't let him get more than a few feet before I run and leap into his arms, peppering his face with kisses.

Wes laughs as I grip his stubbled cheeks, kissing his tired eyelids, his strong brows, his straight nose, and smooth forehead, and it's a sound I never thought this house would hear again.

"I love you," I declare between kisses.

"Love you more," Wes says before intercepting my lips with his own.

The moment the seam of our mouths meet, I feel as if I've been struck by lightning. I'm rooted to the earth through his strong body, captured and suspended in his glowing, buzzing stream of electricity. I grip his face harder as the current courses through us—blinding and devastating and healing and hot—and Wes angles his head to take me deeper, using my mouth as a vessel for everything left unsaid.

He kisses me feverishly, impatiently. As if he has more love to give me than time.

And that's when it hits me.

I know this kiss.

I know this kiss all too well.

Wes

I KNEW FROM THE moment I first laid eyes on Rainbow Williams that I would end up dying for her. I didn't want to believe it, I didn't know how or why, but when Rain needed help, God gave me a gun with a single bullet, a dirt bike, and a clear highway all the way to Franklin Springs. Out of all the sad sacks of shit he could have chosen for the job, he picked me, and for that, I'll be eternally grateful.

I just wish that fucker would have let me have more time with her. But, he's never given a shit about what I wanted before. Why start now?

When I first hear the rumble in the distance, I slow our kiss, pulling her soft body to me even tighter. I memorize every curve, every sigh, and I smile.

"I found a stash of cash in a tackle box in your parents' closet," I murmur against her lips. "It should be enough to keep the lights and water on until you can find a job."

"Wes?"

"And there's extra ammo in your dad's sock drawer." Holding her up with one arm, I snake a hand between us and pull the revolver out of my holster. "Keep this on you at all times. Sleep with it under your pillow, okay?"

I tuck the muzzle into the back of her jeans and pull her tank top down over it.

"Wes, you're scaring me."

The bump and crunch of tires over gravel signal that our time is up. Two car doors slam, followed by a third.

Rain's bright blue eyes go wide, and I hate the panic I see in them.

"Hey." I grab her face like I did during the execution today, forcing her to look at me. "It's okay. You're gonna be okay."

"What's gonna be okay? What's happening, Wes?" Rain's shrill voice is drowned out by an authoritative *bang, bang, bang* on the door.

"Georgia State PD. Open up!"

Rain shrieks and covers her mouth with her hands.

"We have the premises surrounded! Open up!"

"Oh my God, Wes! I have to hide!" she whispers under the sound of more pounding, her eyes darting all over the room.

"No, baby," I shush her, grabbing her face again. "They're not here for you. You did nothing wrong. Just promise me you won't go back to Bitchass Park, okay?" I give her a phony smile. "Stay here. You're safe here."

"What's happening, Wes?"

The banging intensifies to the point that I'm afraid they're going to break Rain's new goddamn door down.

"It's open!" I yell, holding her stare as long as I can.

The door flies open behind her, and in walks a brick shithouse of a cop, followed by the bitch who called them.

"That's him," she declares, pointing a righteous finger in my direction. "That's the man who procured the antibiotics."

Rain spins around at the sound of her voice, shock and betrayal twisting her beautiful features. "Mrs. Renshaw! What are you doing?"

Rain turns to the officer and spreads her arms wide, as if she can single-handedly protect me from the law. "It was me!" she shrieks. "Take me! I gave him the antibiotics! Not Wes!"

The cop flashes Carter's mother a questioning look as I walk around Rain's outstretched arms and kneel before her. Her teary eyes drop to mine, and her fingers thread into my hair as she shakes her head from side to side.

"No ..."

"It was me. I saved Quinton Jones's life." My words are directed at the cop, but my eyes are holding Rain's heartbroken stare. "And even if it wasn't, you can't execute her ..."

I press a kiss to Rain's belly and smile, knowing that a part of me will live on with her forever.

"She's pregnant."

Wes and Rain's story continues in
Dying for Rain.

PLAYLIST

THIS PLAYLIST IS A collection of songs that I either mentioned in *Fighting for Rain* or that I felt illustrated a feeling or a scene from the book. I am grateful to each and every one of the brilliant artists listed below. Their creativity fuels mine.

You can stream the playlist for free on Spotify: https://open.spotify.com/user/bbeaston

"A Little Death" by The Neighbourhood
"Alligator" by Of Monsters and Men
"Alive with the Glory of Love" by Say Anything
"Alone Together" by Fall Out Boy
"Baby Girl, I'm a Blur" by Say Anything
"Back to Your Love" by Night Riots
"coachella" by lovelytheband
"Dream" by Bishop Briggs
"Everyone Requires a Plan" by The Lumineers
"Explode" by Patrick Stump
"Flawless" by The Neighbourhood
"Green Eyes" by Coldplay
"It's a Process" by Say Anything
"Let the Flames Begin" by Paramore
"Mean" by Taylor Swift
"Nervous" by K.Flay
"Numb Without You" by The Maine

"Rainy Girl" by Andrew McMahon in the Wilderness
"Simple Song" by The Shins
"The Archer" by Taylor Swift
"The Only Exception" by Paramore
"watch" by Billie Eilish
"When It Rains" by Paramore
"when the party's over" by Billie Eilish

BOOKS BY BB EASTON

STAND-ALONE ROMANTIC COMEDY

Hilarious. Honest. Hot as hell.

44 Chapters About 4 Men: A Memoir

THE 44 CHAPTERS ABOUT 4 MEN PREQUEL
SERIES

Darkly funny. Deeply emotional. Shockingly sexy.

SKIN (Knight's backstory, Book 1)
SPEED (Harley's backstory, Book 2)
STAR (Hans's backstory, Book 3)
SUIT (Ken's backstory, Book 4)

THE RAIN TRILOGY

A gritty, suspenseful, dystopian love story.

Praying for Rain
Fighting for Rain
Dying for Rain

FOR UPDATES ON NEW RELEASES, SALES, AND
GIVEAWAYS, SIGN UP AT
WWW.ARTBYEASTON.COM/SUBSCRIBE

ACKNOWLEDGMENTS

Ken, every good thing I have, I have because of you. This family, this home, this career that I love so much, this fridge full of premade lunches, this freshly cut grass. You quietly and systematically make all of my dreams come true while I run around frantically and manically dreaming up new ones. Wes thinks God sent him to save Rain, and I think God (or the universe or whatever the hell that thing is that you don't believe in) sent you to save *me*. I love you so much.

To **my mom, Ken's mom, and his sister**—Thank you for never hesitating to watch our kids so that I can try to find that ever-elusive work-life balance thing everyone's always talking about. I'm so incredibly lucky to have your love and support, and so are Baby BB and Mini Ken.

To my content editors, **Karla Nellenbach** and **Traci Finlay,** and my copy editors, **Jovana Shirley** and **Ellie McLove**— Thank you for always treating me like the fragile, delicate flower that I am as you hold my hand and walk me through the emotional minefield that is editing. Not only are you excellent at what you do, professional, and prompt as hell, but you also handle my sensitive little artist heart with care, and I love you for it.

To my beta readers and proofreaders, **Tracey Frazier, April C., Sara Snow, Sammie Lynn, Rhonda Lind,** and **Michelle Beiger DePrima**—It never ceases to amaze me the way you guys put your lives on hold to read my babies. Giving someone your time and attention is an expression of love, and what you do for me is nothing short of that. Thank you.

To my publicist, **Jenn Watson,** and the rest of the team at **Social Butterfly PR**—Thank you for always being there, whether I need you to help me spread some good news at a moment's notice or need some Advil and an Uber after a long night of bad choices. You guys are absolute rock stars. (And I should know—I've seen you do karaoke.)

To my agents, **Flavia Viotti, Meire Dias, Maria Napolitano,** and the rest of the team at **Bookcase Literary Agency**—Thank you for being as excited about my books as I am. It's so nice to work with a team of people who share my vision. I can't wait to see where we go next!

To **Larry Robins** and **J. Miles Dale**—Thank you for changing my life. I can't wait to squeeze you both on the red carpet. Netflix, baby! You did it!

To **Stacy Rukeyser**—I know you're not involved in this project, but I want you to know that I think you're amazing.

To **Colleen Hoover**—I plan on mentioning you in every book I ever write. So … hey, girl!

To **all my author friends**—Thanks to you, I don't have competitors; I have coworkers. I'm not isolated; I'm inundated with love and support. You share with me your time, your advice, your encouragement, your resources, and often, your platforms to help me succeed in an oversaturated market where so very few do. Thank you for letting this pink-haired, foul-mouthed, new kid sit with you. I love you, and if I can ever lend a hand, let me know!

To **the girls (and a few boys) of** #TeamBB—Thank you for the gorgeous Instagram teasers, the Facebook shares, the five-star reviews that never fail to make me cry, the thoughtful gifts, and the tireless pimping you've showered me with over the years. It is because of *you*, forcing your friends and book clubs and sisters and significant others to read my books—oftentimes under the threat of physical violence—that I've been able to pursue this dream at all. I'm humbled by your rabid, relentless support and proud to call you all friends.

ABOUT THE AUTHOR

BB Easton lives in the suburbs of Atlanta, Georgia, with her long-suffering husband, Ken, and two adorable children. She recently quit her job as a school psychologist to write books about her punk rock past and deviant sexual history full-time. Ken is suuuper excited about that.

BB's memoir, *44 Chapters About 4 Men*, and the spin-off *44 Chapters* novels are being adapted into a steamy, female-centered dramedy series for Netflix called *Sex/Life*. Coming late 2020 or early 2021.

The Rain Trilogy is her first work of fiction. The idea, fittingly, came to her in a dream.

If that sounds like the kind of person you want to go around being friends with, then by all means, feel free to drop her a line. You can find her procrastinating at all of the following places:

Email: authorbbeaston@gmail.com

Website: www.authorbbeaston.com

Facebook: www.facebook.com/bbeaston

Instagram:
www.instagram.com/author.bb.easton

Twitter: www.twitter.com/bb_easton

Pinterest: www.pinterest.com/artbyeaston

Amazon: author.to/bbeaston

Goodreads: https://goo.gl/4hiwiR

BookBub: www.bookbub.com/authors/bb-easton

Spotify:
https://open.spotify.com/user/bbeaston

Selling signed books and original art on Etsy:
www.etsy.com/shop/artbyeaston

Giving stuff away in her #TeamBB Facebook group:
www.facebook.com/groups/BBEaston

And giving away a free e-book from one of her author friends each month in her newsletter: www.artbyeaston.com/subscribe

Made in USA - Kendallville, IN
1132522_9781732700741
10.26.2020 1255